Pawsitively
A
Purrfect
Match

Santa Kitty

Santa Kitty

PEPPER MCGRAW

Contents

Chapter 1 — 1

Chapter 2 — 15

Chapter 3 — 29

Chapter 4 — 47

Chapter 5 — 63

Chapter 6 — 85

Chapter 7 — 109

Chapter 8 — 125

Excerpt — 139

Thank you for reading — 151

Other Books by Pepper — 153

Anthologies & Collections — 155

About the Author — 157

One

BYGUL HAD COMPLETELY screwed up a match. It didn't happen often—after all, he *was* the top matchmaking cat at Pawsitively Purrfect Matches. (That wasn't bragging. It was just a fact.)

However, because he was so good at his job, it was even more upsetting when he actually got things wrong—and boy, had he gotten a whole lot wrong with this particular match.

Of course, Bygul had no idea at the time that he'd been given the wrong information, but that was no excuse.

He was still responsible for doing his own research and verifying all the facts, which he had clearly failed to do effectively, which made the entire situation his fault.

He took full responsibility.

This was why Bygul was determined to make things up to the polar bear he'd wronged. All that work to try and match poor Wade Meier to an arctic fox who wasn't even his mate.

Their efforts had probably gotten the polar's hopes up, only to dash them to pieces.

The bear was undoubtedly heartbroken, believing he'd been so close to having a mate, only to lose her to his own cousin.

It was shameful and Bygul was to blame.

His brother Kalyn shared some of the responsibility, of course.

In truth, Kalyn had made the situation much worse.

If Bygul had been there, he would have realized immediately that he had the wrong information and would have changed strategies immediately.

Unfortunately, Kalyn was a bit dense.

So he'd followed Bygul's instructions to the letter, stubbornly clinging to the idea that the fox was meant for Wade and not his cousin Zach.

Of course, Kalyn *was* a cat, and stubbornness did come with the territory.

Even Bygul wasn't immune. Of course, *he* used his stubbornness for the greater good.

It was why he was such a good matchmaker. Well, that and the fact that he'd been trained by the goddess, Freyja, herself, thus ensuring his place as the top matchmaker for Pawsitively Purrfect Matches.

No one had beat his record to date, and undoubtedly, no one ever would.

Because Bygul *never* gave up.

Which meant he was determined to make things right. After all, he'd committed to finding that polar bear a pawsitively purrfect match, and no matter how long it took, Bygul never failed to keep his promises.

Sometimes it took quite a while to find the right match, but this time, Bygul found her almost immediately.

She was purrfect for Wade Meier, though the polar might not agree, at least not at first.

Chances were, the woman wouldn't agree either.

It wasn't because Tessa was human. After all, she'd known about shifters ever since her father mated one when she was little.

And it wasn't because Wade was too stupid to realize she was his mate. Ultimately, he *was* a bear so that was totally expected.

No, the real reason this mating was a challenge was because Wade Meier and Tessa Madison got off on the wrong foot from minute one.

Basically, they hated each other on sight, but it was like Bygul always said: hate was only a swish of the tail away from the glory of love.

Besides, Bygul had a plan involving a number of earthbound cats and one tiny kitten in particular.

This match was going to be purrfect.

Tessa Madison should never have agreed to move in with her cousin and best friend, Keri.

Sure, she'd been in fairly dire straits at the time.

Her asshole boyfriend had cheated on her and unfortunately, their apartment lease was in his name, which meant Tessa was unexpectedly homeless right before the holidays.

Of course, Paul had been willing to let her stay, as part of the "open" relationship he felt was his due. He'd actually expressed shock that Tessa had the audacity to expect monogamy from the man she'd invited into her bed and her body.

What a *dick*.

Shouldn't monogamy be the default expectation? She'd moved in with the man, for goddess' sake. She hadn't thought she needed to explain the parameters of a respectful live-in relationship.

Obviously, if he wanted an "open" relationship, he should have informed her of this before she'd ever moved in. At the very least, they should have had a conversation about it.

According to Paul, though, Tessa was entirely too old-fashioned.

"Everyone's in open relationships now, darling," Paul had informed her. "You've been brainwashed by outdated societal expectations. Open relationships are the wave of the future. If you want to have any sort of relationship this century, you're going to have to accept that fact."

He'd then proceeded to inform her that she was welcome to stay now that she had a clearer understanding of what she could expect from their *modern* relationship.

Tessa, rage so intense she'd been afraid for them both, had simply told him she needed time to process this information and had asked him to give her the day.

He'd agreed, a rather smug look on his face, and had left to spend the day at a buddy's house, no doubt saving them both from disaster, for he'd been seconds away from dismemberment and she from imprisonment.

The moment he was gone, Tessa had called Keri, who'd shown up with half their pack, a rental truck and about a thousand collapsed boxes.

Tessa had then proceeded to take everything she'd paid for out of the apartment.

Everything.

By the time they were done, Paul's apartment was mostly empty except for his ridiculous stereo system and television that spanned the entire wall of their living room.

It wasn't her fault he'd gotten rid of his queen-sized bed when she'd moved in with her deluxe king.

Or that he'd gotten rid of his sagging sofa in favor of her leather sectional.

It wasn't her fault that he hated to cook so only had the bare minimum in supplies until Tessa had moved in with an entire kitchen full of appliances and pretty much every kitchen gadget imaginable.

It took them a while to get everything packed and loaded into the truck, which was why Tessa kept expecting Paul to show up and for there to be a massive confrontation between the local wolf pack and her asshole ex.

She wasn't certain whether she was relieved or disappointed when he never showed.

Either way, she figured it was probably for the best.

She left a note and her key to the apartment on the kitchen counter, right where her espresso machine had stood not long before.

The note had simply said, "The answer is no."

As if he wouldn't have figured that out the minute he walked into the apartment.

She'd wanted to write more, with a stream of profanities, but she'd resisted temptation.

Of course, once everything was out of the apartment, Tessa had nowhere to take it all, so she went online and rented a storage unit not far from her former apartment.

She marveled at the wonders of technology as she downloaded the storage facilities app and opened gates and her unit's garage door from her phone.

Once everything was moved into the unit, without anywhere else to go, she'd ended up following Keri back to her apartment complex, where Keri had somehow managed to convince Tessa to stay in her guest room through the holidays.

"Besides, if I make it through Thanksgiving without bailing on the family, it'll be a miracle," she'd informed Tessa.

Of course, she'd been right.

The minute Keri's mother started nagging her about finding a mate at Thanksgiving dinner, Tessa knew it was all over.

How Aunt Martha never figured out that her harping on Keri's unmated status at Thanksgiving always resulted in her daughter never being around for Christmas, Tessa had no idea.

The minute they got back to the apartment that night, Keri started packing.

"Because she's bad enough on Thanksgiving," she explained while scooping toiletries into a duffel bag, "but Christmas with my mother will drive me mad."

Tessa's response had been a simple roll of the eyes since she knew Keri would be gone for far longer than just the Christmas holiday.

"I won't be back before February," she proved Tessa right by saying next. "So you can take as long as you need to find a new place. Of course, I hope you choose to stay and we can be roommates again, or if not, that you'll move into a different apartment here."

Keri'd been trying to convince Tessa to move into her complex for years.

There was a reason Tessa had always refused though.

Tessa was thoroughly, one hundred percent, depressingly human.

Keri had never held that against her, of course, but Tessa just couldn't imagine living in a shifter-owned apartment complex in the middle of Worcester Falls, surrounded by bears and wolves and other shifters.

Sure, she'd lived with a wolf pack through much of her growing up years, but they were all family in a sense. Worcester Falls, on the other hand, was full of bears—giant, cranky, obnoxious bears—and Tessa, frankly, found them a little intimidating.

When Tessa had been in her teens, she'd had dreams of one day meeting a wolf shifter, who would instantly know she was his mate, similar to what had happened to her dad when he met her stepmom. By the time she'd graduated from college, though, she'd been pretty certain that wish was not going to come true.

As a result, she'd moved to Pleasantville, a decidedly human town, as a means of keeping herself grounded in reality. She was *human* and needed to remember that, rather than allowing herself to get caught up in fantasy dreams that had little basis in reality.

Pleasantville wasn't far from Greensboro, where the pack lived, or from Worcester Falls, where Keri had settled to get some distance from the pack, so it served Tessa well, allowing her to stay connected with the people she loved while also providing enough distance to accept what would never be.

Of course, accepting had led her to Paul the dick and her latest circumstances, living in a town she'd always avoided, in her best friend's apartment, surrounded by predators on all sides.

Keri, of course, had insisted everyone in Worcester Falls was "super-nice" and that Tessa would be perfectly safe there, but Tessa wasn't entirely sure.

Especially after meeting the polar bear who lived across the hall.

He'd hated her on sight, though Tessa had no idea why, and honestly didn't care, because it was better that way.

Better because Tessa had been instantly attracted to the rude bear whose level of hotness could not be overstated.

She hated that she'd noticed him at all and worse that she'd been so busy checking him out the first time she'd seen him, it had taken her several moments to realize he hadn't been at all interested in returning the favor.

Instead, he'd been glaring daggers at her.

Rather than feeling embarrassed that he'd caught her checking him out, she'd been annoyed.

Men had been ogling women for centuries, yet somehow this bear took offense because she'd had the audacity to do the same to him.

Just the thought of the hypocrisy annoyed her every time she remembered that moment, which was why whenever they encountered each other since, she'd taken great joy in glaring daggers right back at him.

This non-speaking, glare-filled relationship of theirs was

a little more than a month old when Christmas morning finally arrived.

WADE MEIER WAS EXHAUSTED.

The week before Christmas was always non-stop parties and endless rounds of drinks at his family's restaurant, The Ice Box.

Wade managed the bar at the restaurant, which meant he worked the later shifts and during Christmas week, those shifts went even later than usual.

This meant he was horribly cranky and groggy when someone started pounding on his door Christmas morning.

He'd think it was his bear relatives—brothers or cousins—or even the arctic foxes, but any one of them would have knocked a whole lot louder, which was saying something because whoever was at his door was determined and loud enough to make his head ache.

He tried to ignore it, but they just kept knocking.

Finally, with a roar of true frustration, he flung off his blankets, dragged on a pair of jeans and stormed toward the front door.

He flung it open and roared, "What?" in the startled face of his very human neighbor.

"Your kitten escaped," she snapped, not seeming at all intimidated by his roar.

"What are you talking about?"

"This kitten. It's cold out here. You need to be more careful."

He blinked bleary eyes at her, trying to get them to focus on the tiny form she was shoving in his face. "That's a kitten."

"I just said that. She's been sitting right here, on your doorstep, patiently waiting for you to let her inside."

He blinked some more at the kitten. She was entirely too small to be either Kahlua or Amaretto and was also the wrong color. "It's a brown tuxedo kitten."

"Huh?" She pulled the kitten back to take a look. "I mean, I guess so. Are tuxedos brown?" She waved a hand as if to dismiss the question. "No matter. The point is, it's *your* brown and white tuxedo kitten. So here."

She shoved the kitten at him again and this time, out of pure reflex, he caught the little one in his hands.

He stared down at her, charmed in spite of himself when she immediately started purring. He was so distracted, he almost missed the woman attempting to walk away. "Hey! Where do you think you're going?"

"It's Christmas morning." She whirled to glare at him. "I have better things to do than care for your misplaced, neglected kitten."

He scowled and pulled the kitten closer to his chest as if he might be able to protect her from the human's callous words. "You're in cahoots with my cousin, Zach, aren't you?"

She looked confused. "What?"

He lifted the kitten to stare at its neck. "There's no tag. What about a note?"

"Huh?"

"Was there a note? Maybe one that said, 'This cat's for you?'"

"What are you talking about? Of course, there wasn't a note."

"Well, there should be one because it's not my kitten."

"Are you sure?"

He gave her an exasperated look. "Yes, I'm quite certain this kitten does not belong to me, no matter what Zach may have told you." He glared at her suspiciously. "What about you?"

"What *about* me?" She looked shocked. "It's not *my* kitten. I don't even live here. I'm just housesitting for Keri. Besides, the kitten was on *your* doormat. Obviously it belongs to you."

"Or maybe you put it there. On purpose."

"Are you serious right now? Where would I get a kitten and *why* would I dump it on your doorstep?"

"Two words. Zach. Meier."

She shook her head. "Never heard of him."

He scowled. "Well, since you found the kitten, I guess that means *you* get to keep her." He stalked across the hall and dumped the kitten back into the woman's hands. "If you need help figuring out how to care for her, you can call Zach's sister Isana, who now that I think about it, is probably the mastermind behind all of this."

"The mastermind behind what? And I told you. I don't know who this Zach person is, so how would I know where to find his sister?"

"Yeah, right." Wade stalked back into his apartment, shutting the door behind him, but then he just stood there, actually *worried* about the kitten.

Letting out a low growl, he turned and looked through his peephole.

His neighbor was pacing up and down the hall between their two doors, a scowl on her face.

As she made a turn and paced back the way she'd just walked, he could see she was cuddling the kitten close to her chest with one arm, while waving the other and ranting.

Great.

He'd left the kitten in the care of a crazy human.

Two

"WELL, THAT DIDN'T exactly go well," Tivali observed.

"Not at all," Muezza agreed.

Ugh. Bygul hated it when his former trainees, now junior matchmaking sidekicks, witnessed his best-laid plans going awry.

"I bet you chose the wrong mate for Wade *again,*" Soraya said to Bygul. "You're not exactly on a winning streak here with that bear. Maybe you should give up trying to identify his mate and leave it to the expert."

"And what expert would that be?" Bygul glared at Soraya. "The only expert around here is—"

"Me, of course!" Soraya exclaimed. "I'm really good at identifying the right mate and I'm pretty certain Tessa doesn't qualify, at least not for Wade Meier."

Ugh. This was the worst part of screwing up. It always

gave Soraya a ridiculous amount of confidence in her own idiotic ideas.

"Oh, *you're* the expert," Muezza said. "Like when you thought Sarah would be a good match for Mason?"

Bygul snorted at the memory of Soraya's conviction the shy wolf was the perfect match for the demanding, grumpy bear.

"Or that Wyatt was meant for Jennifer?" Tivali demanded.

"I don't know what you both are going on about," Soraya said. "I was just exploring the possibilities, that's all. It's what a good matchmaker does."

Bygul let out a huff of exasperation. "A good matchmaker doesn't give up at the first sign of difficulty. A good matchmaker never gives up on his or matches, and let's be clear: Wade Meier *and* Tessa Madison are both our matches now. So we either have to match them with each other or find a different match for each of them. Either way, we're not giving up on either one."

Soraya let out a tiny hiss. "Fine. I suppose we can work on finding her a match too, but I'm not sure she deserves our help. After all, she didn't seem all that enamored with the kitten."

"But she didn't abandon her either," Muezza reminded her.

"Yeah, not like Wade who refused to take her in. If anyone doesn't deserve a match, it's him for ignoring the kitten," Tivali said.

"He's pretty much taken responsibility for half the cats at The Ice Box," Bygul said, "so he's definitely worthy. We're just going to have to figure out a way to get the two of them together. I still say the kitten is the perfect strategy. They can bond over her care."

"You may be a bit optimistic with your hopes there, Bygul," Soraya said.

"Eh, it was probably just poor timing. I should have waited until after Christmas to deliver the kitten, but I was too impatient."

"Well, what are we supposed to do now? They've gone off to entirely different Christmas celebrations," Soraya said.

"I say we follow the kitten," Tivali said.

"Well, then, I guess we'll be celebrating Christmas with the wolves," Bygul said.

"What?" Tivali exclaimed.

"Why?" Muezza demanded.

"She's a human, not a wolf," Soraya wailed.

Bygul smirked. Things were definitely looking up.

WITH NO SUPPLIES TO CARE FOR A KITTEN IN Keri's apartment and the asshole bear refusing to take responsibility for her, Tessa ended up taking the kitten with her to her parents' home.

Walking into that den off insanity always made her smile.

She had no idea why Keri hated spending Christmas with the family.

Okay, so Aunt Martha was a bit much with her desire to have everyone in the pack happily mated, but there was no lack of potential victims on Christmas morning. The entire pack came together for the celebration and it was always amazing.

Sure the wolves were absolutely insane, something that had taken Tessa and her dad, both of them entirely human, a bit of time to acclimate to, but wolves were also hilarious and outrageously fun.

Tessa had only been nine years old when her dad met and fell in love with a wolf shifter.

Their mating happened super-fast, as was apparently typical of shifters when finding their mates, and so, from one day to the next, Tessa had gone from a family of two, consisting of herself and her dad, to being part of an unruly wolf pack.

Technically, Tessa and Keri were step–cousins, but they never bothered much with the step part of that word since they'd bonded from the start, best friends from pretty much the moment they met.

For that matter, Tessa didn't really think of Alexa as her stepmom either. She'd never really known her birth mother, who had died when Tessa was barely a year old, which meant when Alexa came into their lives, Tessa had been more than ready for a mother figure.

After nine years of holidays spent with just her dad, having a mother and an entire wolf pack to celebrate them with was a gift like none other, one Tessa would never take for granted. She knew her father felt the same way.

Keri, probably because she'd been part of the pack her entire life, didn't have the same love for it that Tessa did, which undoubtedly explained why she took off traveling every December and January.

"Hey, Tessa brought a kitten to the feast," her sixteen-year-old brother, Alan, hollered when she walked in the front door of their parents' house.

Tessa scowled at him. "Not funny. That makes it sound like I brought her to be eaten."

"You mean you didn't?" He widened his eyes and gave her a very wolfish grin.

"Knock it off, Alan," their fourteen-year-old sister shoulder-checked him to the side and held out her hands to Tessa. "Can I hold her please?"

Tessa shrugged and held the kitten out to Amaya.

The kitten had been mostly docile the entire time Tessa had her. During the drive to Greensboro, the kitten had explored the car, then had climbed up to sit on the headrest behind Tessa. She'd propped her front paws on Tessa's shoulder and had seemed content to hang out there, watching the scenery race by.

When they'd arrived at her parents' house, Tessa had

scooped the kitten into her arms and carried her inside without any issues at all.

The moment Tessa tried to pass her over to Amaya, however, the kitten became a hissing maniac.

Tessa was so startled, she dropped the kitten, who landed on her feet and darted into the living room, where she was greeted with exclamations and one very wolfish howl of surprise.

Tessa was pretty sure that howl was from her twelve-year-old brother, Matt.

"Don't scare her!" Tessa exclaimed as she hurried into the living room where a number of her family members were gathered, talking.

"Tessa," Aunt Martha exclaimed the moment she saw her. "How are you, sweetheart?"

Oh, great.

An enthusiastic greeting from Alexa's sister, Martha, was always grounds for suspicion. In other words, Tessa had just been doomed to take Keri's place on the holiday's matematching agenda.

"Any new boyfriends, girlfriends, sexy friends at all?"

"Aunt Martha," several cousins groaned.

"What? My only daughter's dedicated to depriving me of grandkids, but Tessa's so much more polite than Keri. You're not going to disappoint me, are you? You're going to find the perfect mate and give me grandnieces and nephews, right?"

Tessa just rolled her eyes and headed for the couch. A

quick check underneath it and all the other furniture in the room revealed no kitten whatsoever.

Tessa stood, hands propped on her hips, and snapped, "All right. Who stole the kitten?"

Everyone turned and stared at her great-uncle Charlie. He was in the recliner, which was completely tilted back as far as it would go, which basically meant he was pretty much horizontal.

"Shit. Those things are death traps for cats." Tessa headed for Charlie, worried the kitten might already be up in the guts of the recliner when she stumbled to a stop. The kitten was curled up in the crook of Charlie's arm, sound asleep.

As was Charlie.

Before she could decide whether to rescue the kitten from Charlie or just leave her there, Martha took hold of Tessa's arm and pulled her from the room, chatting the entire way. "So, I was thinking you would be the perfect one to help. You know Keri so well, I have no doubt that you can help identify her mate. She's just being stubborn at this point."

"Or maybe she hasn't met him yet," Tessa said.

"I'm sure she has or if she hasn't, it's because she's not looking hard enough. So what do you think? You've been staying at her place. Are there any eligible mates in the complex?"

Much to Tessa's dismay, the grumpy polar bear neighbor's face immediately came to mind.

"There is! I can tell. Who is it? Tell me everything." Martha dragged Tessa into the crowded kitchen where her stepmom, Alexa, and a number of aunts and cousins were busy cooking.

"Tessa!" Keri's brother, Cory, cheered her name from where he was busy stirring something on the stovetop.

"Sweetheart!" Alexa, whirled from where she was chopping vegetables, set down her knife and hurried to give Tessa a hug. "Did I hear your brothers talking about a kitten you brought?"

"Yeah. She's sound asleep on Charlie's belly. She freaked out when Amaya tried to hold her."

Alexa shook her head. "That girl. I swear, she gets more like an alpha wolf every day."

"Well, she does come by it naturally," Tessa snickered.

"Who comes by what naturally?" Her father appeared in the back door, a giant platter of meat in his hands. He grinned at Tessa, set the platter on the table, hooked an arm around her neck and dragged her close for a hug. "How's my darling girl?"

Tessa hugged him back. "I'm good, Dad. Happy to be celebrating another Christmas with this crazy clan."

He chuckled. "So what's this I hear about a kitten?"

Tessa explained again, this time with more detail about how she'd come by the kitten in the first place, and left it to Alexa, the alpha wolf of their pack, to explain to her mate that his youngest daughter had intimidated a kitten with her alpha gamma rays.

He let out a booming laugh at that description. "So that's what you were talking about. I agree, Tessa mine, she *does* come by it naturally." He sent a look that was somehow both leering and besotted Alexa's way.

Tessa rolled her eyes, both charmed and disgusted at the familiar display of affection between her parents.

"Never mind about the kitten or Amaya. Everyone knows that girl is going to be alpha someday, so that's not news at all," Martha said. "I'm waiting to hear more about this potential mate for my Keri." She reclaimed Tessa's arm and dragged her to the kitchen table where she claimed two seats for them both, then leaned toward Tessa and said, "Right. Tell me everything."

"Wait. What are you talking about?" Alexa joined them at the table.

"Excellent, Alexa can help too!" Martha exclaimed.

Oh, great. With both their moms working together, Keri didn't stand a chance. She'd probably be mated to that bear before she even returned from her vacation.

"There's an eligible shifter at Keri's complex and I want to know all about him." Martha turned back to Tessa. "Okay, hit me with all the details."

Tessa just stared at her. "I got nothing."

"Oh, come on, Tessa. Even I can see you're not telling the truth on that one," Cory observed from across the room.

Tessa rolled her eyes. "Fine, but I'm telling you there's not much to share. He's kind of a jerk. No, he *is* a jerk. No kind of about it."

"Oh, he can't be that bad," Martha said. "Now tell me, has Keri met him yet?"

"I imagine so. He lives right across the hall from her."

"Wait." Cory swung around from where he stood at the stove. "Are you talking about the smokin' hot polar bear?"

Tessa raised an eyebrow. "You've met him?"

"Oh, honey." Cory waved a hand in front of his face like he was trying to cool down. "Whew. That man is dangerously hot."

"Now we're talking," Martha crowed. "Wait. Does this mean he's a better match for Cory than for Keri?"

"I wish," Cory said emphatically. "Unfortunately, that man does not set off my gaydar even one tiny bit."

"Excellent!" Martha exclaimed. "I mean, not for you, Cory, but it's excellent news for Keri. So tell us all about him, Tessa."

Tessa shrugged. "I really don't know that much, other than he's a jerk."

"I do," Cory said, "and I can tell you right now, Keri's not his mate."

"How do you know that?" Martha demanded.

"Because she'd know, wouldn't she? If they met at all, and they did, so it's pretty obvious, he's not."

"Oh, please," Martha said. "Your sister's stubborn. She'd deny her fated mate just to spite me."

Tessa snickered. "Come on, Aunt Martha. She's not that bad."

"So tell us more about this bear," Alexa said. "What makes him perfect for Keri?"

Tessa stared at her mother incredulously. "I never said he was perfect for anyone. In fact, I said he was a jerk."

"You know what they say, honey," Martha said. "Some jerks make the best bedmates."

"They do not say that," Tessa said.

"*No one* says that," Cory agreed.

"Well, they should," Martha said.

"You seriously want to try and set your daughter up with a massive jerk?" Tessa demanded.

"No, I want to set my daughter up with a hot polar bear shifter who will mate her and make lots of cute babies with her."

Alexa giggled. "I think that sounds like a wonderful plan. What makes him such a jerk, Tessa?"

"You mean besides glaring at me every time he sees me?"

"Oh, he does not," Cory said.

"He does! And he yelled at me this morning."

"What happened this morning?" Martha asked.

So Tessa explained the confrontation she'd had with the polar bear, only to receive no sympathy from any of them.

"So basically," her mother said, "you knocked on your neighbor's door at nine in the morning on a holiday."

"A neighbor who works nights," Cory said.

"How do you know that?" Tessa demanded.

"I've seen him at The Ice Box. He's the bar manager

there and more often than not, he's the one closing down the bar *and* restaurant."

"So he probably worked late and you woke him up at the crack of dawn," Martha said.

"He had a kitten on his doorstep. What was I supposed to do? Ignore it?"

"And then you accused him of neglecting a kitten that wasn't his and then tried to make him take responsibility for it," Alexa said.

Tessa let out a huff of annoyance. "Well, when you put it like that, it doesn't sound that great, but he's hated me from the minute he saw me. Always glaring and growling when he passes by."

"Wait. He growls at you?" Cory exclaimed.

She shrugged. "Yeah. Why?"

"What have you been doing that's so upsetting to his bear?" Alexa asked.

"What am I—are you kidding me right now? I'm just walking along, minding my own business, going into Keri's apartment and he glares at me, growls at me and then ignores me. He's a jerk, that's why his bear's getting upset and it has nothing to do with anything I've done."

"Hmm. I think we should meet this bear," Martha said.

"Absolutely," Alexa agreed.

"Oh, I think that's a terrible idea," Cory said. "I'll definitely be coming along for this excursion."

"Cory!" Tessa exclaimed. "You're not helping!"

"I'm sorry. Was I *supposed* to be helping?"

Three

SOMETHING SOFT BATTED at Tessa's cheek and woke her the morning after Christmas.

"Meow."

Tessa opened her eyes and stared at the brown and white face hovering above her.

"Meow." The kitten lifted her white paw from where it had been resting on Tessa's cheek and patted her with it again. "Meow."

"What do you want?"

"Meow," the kitten repeated.

"Sorry to break it to you, but I don't speak meow." Tessa waited to see if the cat would reply.

"Meow."

"Meow what?" Okay, this was ridiculous. Barely twenty-four hours after finding a kitten and she was already acting crazy, attempting to have a conversation with her.

"Meow." The cat jumped down and ran to the door of Tessa's bedroom, then glanced back at Tessa.

"Are you hungry? Thirsty? Need the litter box?"

The "litter box" consisted of a cardboard box her mom had provided that they'd filled with potter's soil.

Not one of the wolves at her parents' house the day before had ever had a cat for a pet. Imagine that.

They'd all laughed at her when she'd asked.

Tessa sighed and climbed out of bed. "Guess I'm going to have to go shopping later today. Unless we can convince that polar bear to adopt you." She grimaced at even the thought of having to deal with him again.

"Meow."

"All right. I'm up. Let's go see what food we might have in the kitchen."

Tessa had just reached the kitchen when she realized the kitten hadn't followed her there. "Now where'd you go?"

"Meow."

Tessa walked around the kitchen island and peeked down the short hallway leading to the front door. The kitten stood facing it, staring up at the doorknob. "What are you doing over there? I suppose we can knock on the polar's door again, but he might not appreciate it."

At that moment, a loud knocking cut through the quiet of the apartment.

Tessa jumped, but the kitten didn't move from her position at the front door. "Meow." This time the meow was clearly directed at whoever stood on the opposite side of the door.

Tessa sighed as they knocked again. "Who do you think that is, huh?" She scooped up the kitten before opening the door.

She barely held back a groan when she saw who stood there.

HAVING WORKED A RIDICULOUS NUMBER OF HOURS over the past week, Wade was thrilled to have the day after Christmas off. He planned to sleep and do absolutely nothing the entire time.

So he wasn't happy when his slumber was interrupted by a very loud knocking.

He tried to ignore it, but it was so loud, he knew it had to be a shifter.

With a growl of anger, he stormed toward the front door, planning to open it and roar at whoever had the audacity to knock on his door so early in the morning.

He'd almost reached the door when he realized they weren't knocking on *his* door. They were knocking on a *neighbor's* door.

Damn shifters.

He couldn't believe how loud some of them were.

He reached the door and peeked through the peephole just as the knocking started up again.

Wolves.

He could tell by the scent.

It was so strong it filled the entire hallway and was now infecting his own den.

He let out a growl of annoyance.

The three wolves in the hallway turned and faced his door.

They'd been knocking on the human's door. Technically he supposed it was a wolf's door, but the wolf was out of town, leaving the annoying human inside all by herself, surrounded by predators.

Before he could decide whether he should open his door and warn the wolves away, the human threw open hers.

The three wolves turned to face her.

The human scowled at them. "What are you guys doing here?" Wade's shifter hearing not only caught her words, but also the annoyance saturating them.

"We're here to meet the bear, of course!" One of the she-wolves said.

Wade scowled. She'd better not be referring to him.

"Are you kidding me right now?" The human demanded.

The two she-wolves shoved their way forward into the human's space.

The human stepped back—second mistake there, first

being that she'd opened the door at all—and all three wolves filed past her into the apartment.

The human scowled at his door—maybe she sensed him watching—then turned and slammed her door behind her.

Whatever the wolves and human spoke about next, they were too far away for Wade to hear them, which was just fine with him.

Fine!

He wasn't worried about the little human who had no claws or fur or fangs to defend herself against a bunch of rangy wolves.

Not at all!

Though she'd had the kitten in her arms when she answered the door, so perhaps he should worry about the cat.

Nah.

Cats were smart. If need be, he had no doubt the kitten would scale the walls or hide in a tiny space the wolves couldn't reach.

It was the human who was too stupid to realize she'd let predators into her apartment.

But that wasn't his problem and he refused to worry about it.

Refused!

Tessa couldn't believe it when she opened the door and found Alexa, Martha and Cory waiting for her.

This was not good.

She hoped to head them off at the pass, but they just barreled their way inside, demanding to meet the bear.

She closed the door and followed them into the living room. "What bear?"

Cory let out a snort of laughter, amusement written all over his face.

Tessa glared, trying to communicate that she would have her revenge sooner or later.

He just grinned unrepentantly.

"The eligible one, of course!" Martha exclaimed. "The neighbor bear we're going to set up with Keri."

"Keri isn't even in town," Tessa said in exasperation. "How are you going to set them up when she's not even here?"

"She'll be back eventually," Martha said, "and the minute she arrives, we'll be ready with her mate."

"That is the most ridiculous thing I've ever heard."

Cory snorted again, the sound almost drowned out by the gasps of her mother and aunt.

"Tessa Madison!" Alexa exclaimed. "Don't be rude."

WADE HAD JUST GOTTEN SETTLED BACK IN HIS BED
and was on the verge of sleep when a pounding started up
again.

He groaned, grabbed his pillow and pulled it over his
head, but it didn't stop the noise.

"What is up with this human?"

He flung his covers back and stormed toward his front
door once again.

This time he didn't bother dragging on a pair of jeans.

It was clearly shifters banging on his neighbor's door
again and he wasn't getting dressed to tell them off. Served
them right!

He'd almost reached the door when he realized this time,
whoever was knocking was doing so on *his* door.

He paused for a second, contemplating the possibility
that it might actually be his mother at the door, then decided
he just didn't care.

He flung open the door and roared, "Why are you
knocking on doors so early in the morning?" in the startled
faces of the shifters he'd just seen enter the human's apartment not thirty minutes before.

"Thank you!" the human exclaimed from where she
stood just behind the three shifters, cradling the kitten in her
arms. "I really appreciate you proving my point."

Wade scowled. Did he want to know whatever point he'd
just proved for her?

No.

He really didn't.

"Go away," he growled at the four of them, "and don't knock on my door again." He started to slam the door closed, but then yanked it open enough to add, "or anyone's door for that matter. Shifters are trying to sleep around here!"

He went to slam the door again, but one of the she-wolves darted forward and shoved.

He was so startled, he stepped back and the next thing he knew, all three wolves had traipsed into his apartment.

He was left staring in stunned amazement at the human across the hall, who didn't look so much surprised as thoroughly resigned.

"I'd tell you to escape while you can, but you're not exactly dressed for the elements." She raised an eyebrow at him. "Of course, I suppose you could always shift when you get outside."

"I blame you for this fiasco," he growled.

"Me? I'm an innocent bystander."

He narrowed his eyes at her. "Innocent, my ass."

"Oh, Mr. Bear," one of the she-wolves sang from the direction of his living room, stretching the word "bear" into two very long and distinct syllables. "We're waiting."

Wade let out a grunt of annoyance. "*What* are they waiting for?"

The human grinned. "Your presence, I'm sure. Go ahead now. Time to entertain your guests."

"They're *not* guests. At best, they're trespassers. At worst, hostile invaders."

She giggled. "Well, then, I wish you luck on ejecting the invaders." She turned back toward her apartment and Wade lunged.

"Oh, no, you don't." He hooked an arm around her torso, lifted and carted her and the kitten into his apartment, slamming the door behind them.

He set her down, then stood in front of the door, blocking any possibility of escape. "You don't get to leave without *them*."

"Meow."

Tessa grinned. "Fine, but you get to hold the kitten." She handed the meowing furball to him, then turned and sauntered into the living room.

"Meow." The kitten rubbed her chin against his chest, reminding Wade that he was standing in his entryway, stark naked.

He contemplated his options.

He could go to his room, shut the door and go back to bed in the hopes they'd all leave while he was sleeping.

Or while in his room, he could pull on a pair of jeans and then confront the invading wolves in his living room.

Or he could just confront them now. After all, *they* were the invaders, not him, and he had every right to dress however he liked in his own home.

So.

Naked it was.

Even though it *was* becoming a bit painful with the

kitten kneading his chest, tiny claws pricking him in a dozen places.

"Oh, Mr. Bear, we're still waiting!"

"Meow." The kitten butted his chest with her head, then rubbed her cheek against him before starting to knead all over again.

He sighed. "I completely agree. No one should be that annoying, but what am I supposed to do? They're in my living room, refusing to leave."

"Meow."

And now he was having a conversation with a cat rather than dealing with the situation.

"You're ridiculously cute, you know that?" He'd have to add calling Isana and yelling at her to his plan for the day.

So.

Call his cousin.

Then do nothing but sleep.

A perfect plan except for the damn wolves hanging out in his living room along with the sexy, annoying human.

"Mr. Bear!"

Wade stamped into the living room and glared at its occupants.

The two she-wolves were lounging on his leather couch, the male wolf was in one of his recliners and the human was perched on the arm of that recliner.

Why was she sitting so close to that damn wolf? There were other options, including a second armchair and a loveseat. Wade scowled at her, then growled, "Why are you there?"

She looked surprised. "Uh, you dragged me in and told me I couldn't leave unless they went with me. Did you already forget? That's rather concerning."

"Not here in my apartment. *There.*" He glared at the wolf who just grinned back at him, an amused look on his face.

"Uh." She looked around the room. "Where else would I be?"

He stormed toward her, hauled her off the arm of the recliner, shuffled her toward the empty loveseat and settled her there, glaring at the wolf the entire time. "There's plenty of seating."

The wolf snickered, but the human didn't respond at all.

He glanced down at her and realized he'd managed to choose the one spot in the room where she'd be in a perfect position to—

Oh fuck.

He swung around and practically raced from the room, storming down the hall and slamming his bedroom door shut.

He dumped the kitten on his bed and grabbed his jeans.

"Really?" He growled at his very inconvenient boner. "She's friends with Calamity Keri, she's obviously a morning person *and* she's annoying. So knock it off already."

His cock refused to cooperate.

"Oh, Mr. Bear!"

That did it.

Wade carefully tucked his deflating cock into his jeans, zipped them up carefully and scowled. "Now what?"

"Meow."

"Shirt or no shirt?"

"Meow." The kitten bounced toward the end of the bed and pounced on one of his socks. She rolled across the bed, rubbing the sock all over her face and clutching it close between her four paws.

The sock was longer than the kitten, but that didn't stop her. She kicked her legs and somehow managed to get the sock into a bundle that she continued to wrestle from one side of the bed to the other.

Wade sighed. "Too damn cute. You're killing me here and I know exactly who's to blame." The human, sure, but Isana definitely. If it was the last thing he did, he was going to get his revenge on his cousin.

"Come along then," he scooped the kitten, sock and all, into his arms and headed back to the living room.

Apparently he'd decided on no shirt.

No socks either considering one was now covered in cat slobber and the other was who-knew-where.

"And I thought that man was hot before," Cory muttered.

"Before what?" Martha asked.

"Before we saw him naked."

"He does look like a very good candidate for providing me with grandbabies," Martha said.

"Ha," Tessa's mother exclaimed. "Are you blind?"

"Huh?"

"Grandnieces maybe, but you should give up on the idea of grandbabies, at least from that particular bear."

Cory snickered.

"What are you talking about, Alexa?"

"Yeah, what is that supposed to mean?" Tessa demanded.

"Oh, please. If you think we didn't notice where your eyes were riveted the minute he set you down on that settee, you're insane." Cory grinned.

Tessa rolled her eyes. "Well, it was right there. In my face. What was I supposed to do?"

"Look away!" Martha exclaimed. "His cock is not for you. I've already claimed it for my daughter."

"Don't be ridiculous, Martha," Alexa said. "You can't claim someone's cock on behalf of someone else."

"Besides, I already told you," Cory said. "That bear is not Keri's mate."

"And I told you that just because she didn't recognize him doesn't mean he's not her mate," Martha said.

"Are you aware that he calls her Calamity Keri?" Cory

asked. "To her face, mind you. He doesn't even keep that shit to himself."

"Really?" Tessa grinned. "Why?"

"Apparently she set off the smoke alarm ten times in the first two weeks after moving in."

"And that would be why Keri's banned from cooking at all family functions," Martha said mournfully. "I was really hoping the bear wouldn't discover her lack of culinary skills until *after* they'd mated."

"I'm still stuck on her setting it off only ten times." Tessa laughed. "Keri must be getting better at using kitchen appliances. Who would have guessed?"

"Eh, I think it has more to do with the fact that the tenth time it happened, the polar bear ripped the smoke alarm off the ceiling and crushed it in his bare hands. He then threatened to maul Keri to a bloody stump if she dared replace it."

"Yeah, that definitely sounds like something the bear would do." Tessa snickered. "I told you guys. He's kind of an asshole."

Cory just stared at her.

"What?"

"Uh, I seem to remember a story about you and Keri your first semester in the dorms as roommates."

"That was entirely different," Tessa said. "We were in serious danger of being torn limb from limb by pretty much everyone in the dorm."

"What did you do, Tessa?" Alexa demanded.

"Well I certainly didn't crush the smoke alarms with my bare hands."

"No," Cory said. "She just removed all the batteries when everyone was sleeping."

Alexa and Martha both gasped.

"That's so dangerous, Tessa!" Alexa said.

"Well, I had to do something. Keri was addicted to popcorn at three in the morning. We replaced seven microwaves our first month in the dorms. If I could have, I would have banned her from the dorm kitchen entirely. Instead we took to keeping back-up microwaves and fire extinguishers in our dorm room, just so that we could replace them immediately."

At that moment, the bear stamped into the living room, kitten in his arms. He set her on the floor and she immediately started rolling around, wrestling with some sort of weird-looking ball of cloth.

Was that a sock?

"Why are you here?" the bear demanded, glaring at the women on the couch.

"To meet you, of course!" Martha jumped to her feet. "It's such a pleasure. What's your name, Mr. Bear?"

He scowled. "Wade Meier and you are?"

"I'm Martha, Keri's mother. This is my sister, Alexa, and my son, Cory. I wanted to invite you to our family dinner this Wednesday night."

Wade looked confused. "Why?"

"Oh, you know, to get to know you better."

"Why?"

"Because you live across from my daughter and my niece, of course."

"Your niece?"

"Tessa." Martha gestured toward her.

"But she's completely human," he said.

Martha scowled. "She's still my niece. So we'll see you this Wednesday, then?"

"No."

"Oh, do you have to work because we could make it lunch?"

"No."

"No you don't have to work or no, lunch doesn't work?"

"Both."

"Well, that's disappointing," Martha said.

"I really like Aunt Martha," Bygul announced. "She's my kind of human."

Tivali let out a huff of amusement. "Of course, she is. She's all about matematching her daughter, which is the kind of thing you live for."

"*We* live for," Soraya said.

"Okay, fine. It's the kind of thing all of us live for," Tivali said.

"I may have to try my hand at matematching this Keri," Bygul said, "assuming her mother doesn't manage it first by stealing Wade from us."

"Oh, please," Muezza said. "There's no way a human could possibly beat us at the matematching game, especially one who happens to be a wolf shifter."

Bygul let out a grunt of exasperation.

"Now you've done it," Tivali said.

"What?" Muezza demanded.

"You've gone and challenged the fates, that's what," Bygul snapped. You'd think cats who worked for the goddesses would know better than to tempt fate with such a blatant challenge, yet there they were.

Challenge issued.

Four

"SO, WADE, TELL us about yourself," the woman with the annoying sing-song voice said.

Martha, she'd said her name was. He wasn't at all surprised to know that Calamity Keri had a mother who was just as annoying as she was.

He glared at Tessa, blaming her for the wolves' presence in his home.

"Cory says you work at The Ice Box," Martha said. "Does that pay well?"

"Mother," Cory groaned.

Tessa snickered.

Wade crossed his arms and transferred his glare from Tessa to the nosy she-wolf.

"I was just wondering," Martha said. "Have to make sure he can afford to buy Keri the latest in shoe fashions."

What the hell was she talking about? Why would he ever buy shoes for her crazy daughter?

Tessa giggled, no doubt entertained by his confusion and annoyance.

"Are there upward mobility opportunities at The Ice Box or are you eventually planning to open your own restaurant?"

"Mother," Cory groaned again. "Would you stop interrogating the man?"

Deciding he'd wasted enough time on this nonsense and that if anyone should be asking questions, it was him, Wade snapped, "Are there upward mobility options where *you* work?"

Martha looked shocked.

Her sister, Alexa, laughed. "Oh, she doesn't have a job, unless you want to call pack meddler a job."

"I beg your pardon," Martha exclaimed. "I prefer the title, pack matematcher."

Wade blanched at that statement, the reason for all her questions and the comment about shoes for her daughter suddenly taking on new meaning.

A terrible meaning.

"That title only works if you actually manage to arrange a mating or two," Cory said. "All you ever do is meddle. I think Aunt Alexa's got the right idea. Pack meddler. It has a nice ring to it, don't you think?"

"Don't you dare spread that title to the rest of the pack, Cory Sampson!"

"It's time for you all to leave," Wade informed them, a bit panicked to realize the crazy woman somehow thought he might be a good match to Calamity Keri.

He couldn't think of anyone he was less inclined to get to know than that terrible menace to society.

Even the annoying human would be more appealing.

He glared at Tessa. "Time. To. Go."

She grinned back at him. "But we're having so much fun."

"And you haven't answered any of my questions," Martha said.

"Okay, time to stop torturing the poor bear." Alexa stood, hauling her sister up with her.

"Fine," Martha sighed, "but I expect to see you at dinner Wednesday night. Tessa can bring you."

Tessa looked horrified at the thought. "Aunt Martha, he's probably busy."

Actually Wade usually had Wednesdays off, though he often went in to handle a few management tasks at some point.

He didn't plan to mention this though, which was why he was shocked to hear himself say, "What time?"

TESSA GASPED, THEN GLARED AT WADE.

He just smirked back at her.

He'd done that just to annoy her! Agreed to go to dinner at her aunt's just so that she would have to bring him.

Talk about cutting off his nose to spite his face. He had no idea how bad Martha could get.

"Seven sharp," Martha said. "Tessa, don't be late."

Cory chuckled, then muttered, "Your funeral, man," as he sauntered by, headed for the door.

Wade had a slightly ill look on his face, but didn't retract his acceptance of the invitation.

"You'll come as well, Cory," Martha said as if her son had ever missed one of their weekly dinners, unlike his sister Keri, who took great pleasure in ditching the family gatherings.

"Oh, I wouldn't miss this dinner for the world." Cory threw a very wolfish grin over his shoulder at Tessa, who glared back, promising retribution with her eyes.

WADE BREATHED A SIGH OF RELIEF WHEN THE door closed behind the wolves and his human neighbor.

"I can't believe they took so long to leave," he muttered, glaring at the door.

"Meow." The kitten rubbed against his legs, then stood on her hind feet, stretching high to knead his jeans.

Wade propped his hands on his hips and stared down at her. "Seriously? I can't believe she left you."

He leaned down and scooped the kitten into his arms.

She'd apparently abandoned his sock in favor of following him to the door.

Now what?

"Meow."

"You are just so darn cute. But you can't stay. That human doesn't get to foist you off on me, no matter how adorable you may be." He opened the door, crossed the hall and pounded on the human's door.

"Well, now, miss us already, did you?" Cory drawled when he opened the door.

Wade scowled and held the kitten out to Cory. "You guys left something behind."

Cory took a giant step back. "Oh, no. I'm not accepting any kittens today. Or ever. Never, that's the word I meant to say. *Never.*"

"YOU FORGOT THE KITTEN."

Tessa looked up to see Wade standing on on the other side of the kitchen island, glaring at her.

He set the kitten down on the floor and she bounded

around the island and immediately attacked one of the dish towels hanging from a cabinet handle.

The towel fell to the floor and the kitten darted away, then darted back and attacked.

The kitten's paws went every which way as she spun the towel and herself on the tile floor.

She was so darn cute.

Tessa was so busy being charmed by the kitten's antics, she almost missed Wade leaving.

"Wait!" She scrambled after him. "The kitten seemed super happy at your place. Don't you think she'd be better off with you?"

"Not a chance. Besides, I already have three cats." He reached the door and swung it open.

Tessa caught the door in her hand and followed him out into the hallway. "What do you mean you have three cats? I didn't see any evidence of cats at your apartment. Where were they? You should take the kitten to play with them. I bet they'd love the company."

"No," he grunted as he reached his door.

"You're lying, aren't you? Making up pets just so you don't have to take care of that poor, defenseless kitten."

He whirled and glared at her. "As if you aren't perfectly aware of Isana's manipulations. Yes, I have three cats and it's all her fault. I refuse to take on another one. So you can just tell her that Wade said no."

"Who the hell is this Isana person and if you really have three cats, where are they?"

"They're at the restaurant. My cousin manipulated all of us into taking on a mother cat and her five kittens."

"I thought you said you only had three cats."

"I do. The mama and two of the kittens are mine. My cousin, Zach, and my brothers, Luke and Steve, were also conned by Isana and have each adopted one of the other kittens."

"So where are they?" Tessa asked suspiciously, not at all convinced he was telling the truth.

"I told you. They're at The Ice Box."

"So they're restaurant kitties?"

He shrugged. "Mine are bar kitties, but sure."

"Do you ever bring them home with you?"

"Nah. The restaurant's their home and I don't think they'd like it if we hauled them back and forth all the time. They didn't exactly enjoy their trip in the carrier yesterday," he muttered.

"Yesterday?"

"My cousin made this big production of hauling all the cats from the restaurant to our family celebration and then gifted them to all of us, as if they were hers to give in the first place. She's a complete hypocrite that one, always talking about never giving pets as gifts, then giving them out left and right when she doesn't have room in her shelter."

"Wait. Your cousin runs an animal shelter?"

"A cat one anyway. She hates dogs, though I guess a local dog rescue's been paying for the use of her kennels, so she's having to deal with them to a certain extent." An arrested look crossed his face. "And I just got a fabulous idea for revenge. Gotta go."

"But wait. What about Mischief?"

"Mischief?"

Great. She hadn't intended to let the name slip. "I mean, the kitten."

"You named her?"

"Not really. I just got tired of calling her the kitten, so I gave her a nickname."

"You know what that means, don't you?"

She scowled at him. "What?"

"She's yours now. Everyone knows if you don't name them, you can still pass them on to someone else, but the minute you give them a name, you're doomed. Enjoy your new life as a crazy cat lady." He opened his door and disappeared inside.

"Hey! One cat does not a crazy lady make!"

WADE GRINNED AT THE OFFENSE IN TESSA'S VOICE as he shut the door behind him.

His grin faded when he caught sight of his mangled sock in the middle of the living room.

Mischief was an excellent name for that kitten.

He couldn't possibly be missing her, could he?

He shook his head.

No.

He already had too many feline responsibilities.

Which reminded him.

It was time to call his interfering cousin.

"I have no idea what you're talking about, Wade," Isana snapped five minutes later.

"Oh, so I'm just supposed to believe that some random kitten happened to show up on my doorstep and you weren't behind it?"

"Are you kidding me right now? I would never just leave a kitten on someone's doorstep. At the very least, she'd be in a carrier and I'd hand her to you in person!"

Hm. She had a point. That's exactly what she'd done the day before—handed him a huge carrier with two kittens and the mama inside.

It was a ridiculously dramatic way to hand over cats he'd already mostly accepted responsibility for.

He let out a growl of frustration. "I can't believe you actually went to The Ice Box and rounded them all up, only to bring them to us so we could then cart them back to The Ice Box."

"Hey, it worked, didn't it? All of the cats are now official restaurant kitties."

"I'll have you know my Amaretto and Kahlua are bar kitties and I'm pretty sure Steve's is a pastry kitten."

Isana snickered. "If I'd known a kitten would mellow Steve out, I'd have gifted him one years ago."

"I don't think anyone could have predicted that turn of events," Wade said dryly. "So let me get this straight. You don't know a thing about this brown and white tuxedo kitten my human neighbor's been trying to pawn off on me."

"Not a clue," Isana said cheerfully. "Obviously you've been in need of more companionship and the universe has seen fit to grant you with endless kittens."

"See, you saying things like that makes me think your hands are all over this situation, so let me be clear: there'd better not be any more kittens showing up on my doorstep, let alone endless ones."

Isana giggled. "Well, I guess that's up to the universe. Good luck, Wade."

"Wait a minute. Isana?"

Great.

She'd hung up on him.

So rude!

Tessa spent the rest of the day after Christmas, shopping with Alexa and Martha.

Cory had plans with friends that afternoon, so he gleefully abandoned her to the whims of his meddling mother and aunt.

And meddling they were.

As they traipsed through stores, searching for the best after-Christmas sales, the two women quizzed Tessa about everything to do with the bear.

It was enough to drive her mad.

Nothing she said discouraged them, though as time went on, it became clear the two sisters weren't exactly in agreement about the perfect mate for the bear.

"How many times do I have to say it?" Tessa demanded. "I'm sure the bear has a perfect mate somewhere. Most shifters do, after all, but whoever that unlucky woman is, it's neither Keri nor me."

"Well, of course, it's not you, darling," Martha said, "but don't get discouraged. We're not giving up on you either. We'll get Keri mated and you're next."

Tessa groaned. "Seriously. It's like you're not even listening."

"Oh, I'm listening, darling." Martha held up a strange-looking creature dressed in a Santa suit. "What do you think?"

"It's the ugliest thing I've ever seen," Alexa said.

"I know! Isn't it perfect? I was thinking I'd put him in the downstairs bathroom. He can sit on the shelf right across from the toilet."

Tessa blanched. "So every guest will have to stare at his ugly face while taking care of business?"

"Hm. That's a good point. I wonder if there's another one around here."

"Another one?" Tessa and Alexa asked in unison.

The look on Alexa's face told Tess it wasn't just her. The creature was the ugliest thing she'd seen in a long time.

"Of course. I wouldn't want the men to miss out on the view, so I'll need one to put on the shelf over the toilet too." She wandered down another aisle, only to cry out in joy and reappear a moment later holding a gnome dressed as an elf.

Tessa really hadn't thought it possible, but the elf-gnome was actually uglier than the Santa-creature.

"Oh, my goddess," Alexa muttered. "I feel faint."

Tessa burst into laughter. "All right, I'm convinced."

"About the bathroom nightmares?" Alexa asked in horror.

"'No. About dinner Wednesday night. I cannot *wait* to hear everyone's opinion of these creatures."

The rest of the afternoon and evening were as ridiculous —and if Tessa was being honest, as entertaining—as the creature conversation.

By the time she got home that evening, Tessa's trunk was full of cat supplies and the occasional holiday finds, which thankfully did not include any of Martha's more atrocious discoveries.

Somehow, Tessa had managed to discourage Martha from buying her the hideous Christmas jumpsuit covered in mistletoe, candy canes and giant snowflakes.

Martha had sworn it would look fabulous on Tessa's figure.

It absolutely didn't.

Tessa knew this because the only way she could convince Martha to leave the damn thing behind was to actually try it on.

Unfortunately, a former classmate happened to be walking by right as Tessa was modeling the hideous thing for Martha and Alexa, and had taken a photo that she'd then posted on social media, tagging Tessa on it.

All it had taken was the accumulation of about two dozen laughing and horrified emojis in the first two minutes to convince Martha the jumpsuit should *not* come with them.

All in all, it had been a fairly successful after-Christmas shopping spree, for Tessa ended up with everything she needed to care for Mischief and nothing she would be too embarrassed to wear out in public, the latter never guaranteed when shopping with Martha.

Tessa spent the evening replacing the cardboard box with actual litter boxes and setting up a feeding station with actual cat food in the kitchen.

She then spent time figuring out which window was the best spot for the perch she'd purchased and extracting a ridiculous amount of cat toys from their packaging.

She tossed each one into a basket Mischief took great pleasure in jumping in and out of, extracting one-by-one each toy Tessa added.

By the time all the toys were out of their packaging, the floor was covered and both Tessa and the kitten were exhausted.

"Time for bed, Mischief." Tessa led the way, unsurprised when the kitten chose to climb onto her bed, rather than making use of one of the many cat beds Tessa had scattered throughout the apartment.

After pacing the bed and kneading the quilt for a while, Mischief climbed onto Tessa's pillow, shoved her nose into Tessa's ear and purred them both to sleep.

"You know, it might be time to get some outside help," Soraya said.

"Excuse me?" Bygul demanded. "I have everything under control. There is no need for outside interference."

"Well," Tivali said, "I'm not seeing much movement in terms of romance, though she is bonding quite nicely with the kitten."

"Yes," Muezza agreed. "Maybe we should just call it good. After all, we matched the kitten and that's always the first goal, right?"

"Of course, it is," Bygul said, "but I'm not giving up on finding Wade Meier his purrfect mate. I owe him and I'm going to make it happen."

"And I'm not saying we should give up," Soraya said. "I'm just suggesting we ask for help."

"Who would you suggest?" Muezza asked. "Because we

all know Kalyn is an absolute disaster."

"Oh, not that idiot," Soraya said. "I'm talking about the Big Guy himself."

Bygul let out a rumble of annoyance. Who the hell was the Big Guy? He was the top matchmaker at Pawsitively Purrfect Matches. There shouldn't be any guy bigger than him.

Tivali snorted. "You're not seriously suggesting—"

"Of course, I am. He's purrfect for this sort of thing."

"Who?" Muezza demanded what Bygul was thinking, but had no intention of asking because that would be tantamount to admitting some other matchmaking cat might be more important than him and that was simply impossible.

"Santa Kitty, of course!" Soraya exclaimed.

"You've got to be kidding," Bygul exclaimed.

"Not that pompous fool," Muezza said. "He's unbearable."

"And an idiot to boot," Tivali said.

"He is not!" Soraya exclaimed. "He's sweet and an excellent matchmaker."

"Where?" Bygul demanded incredulously. "In hell? Because that's the only place I can imagine anyone trusting that maniac to matchmake."

"Oh, he's not that bad," Soraya said.

"Yes, he is," Bygul, Muezza and Tivali chorused.

"In fact," Bygul said. "I'm pretty sure he's much worse than any of us really know."

Tivali nodded. "Undoubtedly."

Five

TESSA WOKE THE second day after Christmas to Mischief's paw patting her cheek once again.

"Is this how it's going to be every morning?" Tessa asked the kitten.

"Meow."

"Well, it is a much nicer wake-up call than my phone's alarm, not that it's going off this week, of course." She'd disabled it the minute her break began and if the kitten remained reliable, she might never activate it again.

"Come along, my darling, let's go get some breakfast."

Tessa and the kitten spent a leisurely morning in front of the television, surfing the internet and playing with cat toys.

Tessa didn't even bother getting out of her pajamas.

It was glorious!

Until a knock came on the door, of course.

She scowled, wondering if she could just ignore it and whoever it was would go away.

They knocked again.

Probably not.

She grabbed her robe, threw it over her pajamas and headed for the front door. She didn't bother tying the belt and instead let it trail behind her.

Mischief chased after it, hooking her claws in it and collapsing on the ground for a free ride.

They had discovered this fun activity the day before and Tessa found it to be as adorable today as she had yesterday while Mischief found it to be just as entertaining.

Throwing open her door, Tessa rolled her eyes when she saw who was waiting there.

"Again?"

"You're not even dressed?" Alexa asked.

"Of course she's not dressed," Cory said, pushing his way inside. "Between shopping and the holidays, this is probably the first day of our break that she's had no plans whatsoever and here we are ruining it for her." He winked at Tessa. "Sorry, doll, but we *are* ruining it." He clapped his hands. "Go get dressed. Chop chop."

Tessa groaned. "Why?"

"Things to do, people to see, places to be."

"That is completely not true," Tessa said even as she stepped back to let her mom and aunt into the apartment.

She slammed the door and followed them into the living room, where she glared at them, hands on hips. "I made no plans, I have no people I want to see and no places I want to be. And since I'm on break, I have no things I have to do, so begone, you evil vacation-ruiners, you."

Alexa laughed. "Oh, come on, darling, you know we wouldn't be here if we didn't have an excellent reason."

Alexa looked at Cory, who just smirked at her.

There was no way they had even a good reason, let alone an excellent one.

An amusing reason, probably, given Cory's sparkling eyes. An entertaining one, undoubtedly, since he'd obviously been willing to give up one of *his* days off for this madness.

An excellent reason, though?

Most definitely not.

WADE WALKED INTO THE ICE BOX AROUND ONE-thirty the following afternoon, not really thrilled to be back at work so soon after the holiday, but actually looking forward to seeing his three cats.

He'd only seen them briefly Christmas evening before bringing them back to the restaurant and he hadn't seen them at all the day before.

He couldn't believe how much he'd missed them.

It was quite ridiculous actually.

Even knowing that, he still couldn't help but grin when

he caught sight of Amaretto and Kahlua wrestling and chasing each other from one bar stool to the next.

Shifters at the tables closest to the bar were laughing and calling out bets to each other about which of the cats was going to win the race.

"I've completely lost track of who's in the lead," a cat shifter complained.

"Eh, it's definitely Kahlua," a grizzly said with a grin.

"I was pretty sure it was Amaretto," a she-wolf said.

"They look exactly alike," her wolf companion said. "They're literally identical."

They weren't, but you did have to examine their markings closely as their marbled coats looked markedly similar.

It had taken Wade days of examining the cats to determine that Amaretto's bullseye markings was just a little lower on his sides than Kahlua's were.

At that moment, a cat flew over the top of the bar and landed on the bar stool between the two kittens.

With the flick of her paw, Bahama Mama sent both of her kittens tumbling to the floor.

Wade chuckled and lifted the sweet tabby into his arms. "Doing your best to keep your kittens out of trouble, huh, Mama? I hate to tell you this, but it's a losing battle."

He walked around the bar and got to work.

"You are kidding me," Tessa exclaimed when she saw where Cory had driven them. "Why are we here?"

"It's the best Shenanigans restaurant in the area!" Martha exclaimed.

Tessa rolled her eyes. "*All* of the Shenanigans are excellent. You just want to visit The Ice Box because of the bear."

"Well, he's definitely a perk," Alexa said. "Come on, darling. We'll have fun."

Tessa didn't believe *that* for a minute.

"You should have told me we were coming here. I would have brought Mischief along."

"Why on earth would you bring a cat to a restaurant?" Cory exclaimed.

"Because they have restaurant kitties here and I don't really have a place to live right now so adopting a kitten isn't exactly smart. I'm trying to convince the bear to adopt her instead."

"Of course, you have a place to live," Martha said. "You're at Keri's."

"Sure, but it's not like I can live there forever and even if I could, it's Keri's apartment. She may not want a kitten."

"Oh, I can guarantee she doesn't," Cory muttered.

"See? Exactly my point."

"Oh, stop dawdling," Martha said. "We're eating here and that's final."

Thankfully when they walked inside, the hostess ended up seating them on the other side of the restaurant from the bar.

That didn't stop Aunt Martha though.

"Could you ask the bear to visit us?" she asked the hostess once they were seated.

The hostess looked confused. "Which bear would that be?"

"There are more than one bears here?" Martha exclaimed.

"Mother, The Ice Box is owned by a bunch of polar bears and arctic foxes," Cory said.

"Well, how was I to know? We're looking for Wade."

"No, we're not," Tessa said. "Feel free to ignore her."

"Tessa!" Alexa admonished.

"What? She's completely out of control."

"I beg your pardon," Martha exclaimed.

Tessa groaned. "You do understand that Keri's a shifter, right? When she meets her mate, she'll know, so you really don't have to obsessively attempt to matematch her."

"Oh, boy," the hostess muttered. "I'll leave you to peruse the menus." She hustled away.

Cory snickered.

"Maybe if we order drinks, Wade will deliver them," Martha said.

"Oh, now that's a terrible idea," Cory said.

"It sure is," Tessa agreed.

Things were bad enough when Martha was sober. If she started drinking—dear goddess!

Tessa shuddered at the thought.

Watching her mother and aunt pore over the drinks menu, Tessa realized she was in serious trouble.

"Sure you don't want that drink?" Cory muttered out of the side of his mouth.

"I'm thinking I may not survive the night without one," Tessa said.

"One, hell," Cory said.

"You're right. I probably need about five. That'll be enough to induce unconsciousness, don't you think?"

Cory snickered. "Lightweight."

"Hey, not all of us have a wolf's constitution, you know."

He grinned. "Yeah, I know."

Tessa had never actually been to The Ice Box before, so she wasn't really sure what to expect, but the food was absolutely divine and she actually ended up enjoying herself quite a bit.

Of course, that didn't stop her aunt from embarrassing her terribly.

First, it turned out their waiter was a polar bear named Luke.

Tessa was pretty certain Wade had mentioned a brother named Luke, but she wasn't going to say that to her aunt, who was busy grilling the poor shifter like a trout.

"So, Luke, have you met your mate yet?" Dear goddess, she didn't even hesitate to put that out there.

Tessa was actually pretty impressed because Luke didn't bolt the minute Martha asked such an invasive question.

"I haven't, no," he said. "What can I get you ladies to start with?"

"That's a shame," Martha said. "My daughter's still looking as well."

Tessa groaned at the same time Cory went into a choking fit.

Luke glanced at Tessa and raised an eyebrow.

"Not me," Tessa quickly assured him. "I'm not her daughter."

He didn't seem surprised, which meant he'd probably scented that she was human.

"No, she's my daughter," Alexa said quickly, "and she's quite single as well."

"Goddess, save me," Tessa groaned.

Cory made a choking sound and his shoulders shook with laughter.

"You suck," Tessa muttered.

"Ah." Their poor waiter seemed speechless. "Drinks?"

"I'll take some water!" Tessa exclaimed then realized they already had water in their glasses, water that was shaking in unison with Cory's shoulders. "I mean, um, oh, shit, I don't know."

"Language, Tessa," Alexa admonished.

"Just bring me something strong," Tessa said.

"No," Cory said. "Bring her something strong for a human, not shifter-strong."

"Right, yes, that."

"Long Island iced tea?" Luke asked.

"Perfect," Tessa said.

"I'll have a Be Were," Cory said.

Tessa rolled her eyes. "Seriously? That's what you're ordering?"

"Hey, I like it."

"How can you possibly like a beer that is so stupid?"

"How can a beer be stupid?" Martha wondered.

"It mocks humans and shifters with that idiotic logo."

Cory grinned. "That's why I like it."

The rest of the night pretty much followed that routine.

Luke brought then their drinks and Tessa quickly claimed Cory's beer so that she cold peel off the label with the insane looking wolf drooling on it, then sucked back her tea and tried to ignore her aunt's increasingly pushy questions.

Luke brought their dinner and by this time, Alexa and Martha had plowed their way through half a bottle of Witches' Brew, which probably wouldn't seem like a lot to most humans, but Tessa knew exactly how potent Witches' Brew was.

Worse was the fact that a bottle of Witches' Brew continually replenished itself. It was horrifically expensive because no one knew how much of the Brew they were going to get in one bottle, but it was always a lot more than the container should be able to hold.

"I can't believe they're drinking that shit," Cory muttered. "It's damn strong, especially for non-witches."

"We're never getting out of here with our pride intact.

You know that, right?" Tessa asked. "Oh, goddess, he's coming back. They are so freaking drunk."

"So," Martha drawled drunkenly as Luke delivered their dinner plates. "I don't suppose you're gay, are you?"

Cory let out a horrified gasp and Tessa giggled at his horror.

"Because my son here happens to be gay and he's also without a mate."

"Really?" Luke set Cory's plate in front of him and winked.

To Tessa's amazement, Cory blushed.

From that moment on, every time Luke visited their table, Martha focused on selling Cory as a potential mate to Luke.

"The biggest downside to mating Cory," Tessa announced as she finished off her third Long Island iced tea, "would be the interfering, meddling mother-in-law you would gain."

"Tessa!" Alexa gasped.

"Eh, she's right," Cory said. "Anyone who wants me is gonna have to put up with all of that." He waved a lazy hand toward his mother, who was obliviously sprawled in her chair, sucking down yet another mug of Witches' Brew.

"Who in the hell is going to drive us home?" Tessa wondered. "It sure isn't gonna be me, because I'm gonna need a fourth one of these." She held up her glass.

Luke grinned. "You got it. And we'll make sure all of you get home safely. All part of the Shenanigans service."

"I thought this restaurant was called The Ice Box," Martha said in confusion.

"Oh, goddess, she's really drunk," Cory muttered.

"It's Shenanigans: The Ice Box, Aunt Martha."

"Well, that doesn't make any sense. Why does it have two names?"

"So you know what you're getting," Luke said. "We can't just call it Shenanigans. What would that tell you? Gas station? Diner? Motel? Who knows what you'd get."

"But The Ice Box says restaurant?" Alexa asked.

Luke grinned. "It not only says restaurant, it says one that's run by arctic shifters."

Martha just looked confused.

"Give it up, man," Cory said. "She's too far gone for any sort of logic."

Tessa giggled.

Luke grinned and started to turn away, but then Alexa exclaimed, "Wait!"

He turned back expectantly.

"Are there any other single shifters around?"

Tessa groaned.

"Well, there's my brother Wade. He's the bar manager. There's my brother Steven. He's the pastry chef. And there are any number of arctic foxes in the kitchen and on the floor, who are unmated." He glanced around. "My cousin, Sheri over there, my cousin Jonathan over there and my cousin Matt, but he's only seventeen."

"Hmm, yeah that's too young for my Tessa."

"Too young for Keri too," Martha popped up. "Good thing we've already settled on Wade for her."

This time both Cory and Tessa groaned.

Luke grinned. "Does Wade know he's been chosen for this honor?"

Cory snickered. "Oh, I'm pretty sure he suspects something, though he may be in denial. I certainly would be."

Tessa giggled. "He has no idea what's coming his way."

For the next hour, she and Cory focused on trying to get their mothers to consume at least some of the food on their plates.

Unfortunately, the women were more interested in the seemingly bottomless bottle of Witches' Brew than they were in the delicious steaks they'd both ordered.

By the time the meal was finished, Tessa felt as if she'd run a gauntlet.

She sent up a prayer of thanksgiving when both Martha and Alexa turned down the offer of desserts.

Her relief, however, was short-lived.

"All right, my loves," Martha said as she slowly swayed to her feet. "It's time for after-dinner drinks in the bar."

Tessa groaned as Martha hauled Alexa to her feet and the two women slowly stumbled their way through the restaurant, headed for the bar.

"Come on," Cory said. "We might as well get it over with."

"Can't we just stay here and pretend we don't know them?"

He raised an eyebrow at her. "I'll remind you that both Wade and Luke know that isn't true. More importantly, do you actually trust our mothers on their own?"

"Congratulations, brother."

Wade looked up in confusion.

Luke stood on the opposite side of the bar, grinning at him.

"What are you talking about?"

"I hear you've met your mate."

What the hell?

Wade didn't know which was worse—the fact that his brother had been told a huge whopper of a lie or that the minute he mentioned mate, Wade's brain immediately pictured the human.

Tessa.

"Who the hell told you that?" Wade demanded.

"I hear her name's Keri."

What the hell? The human's name wasn't—

Goddess, save him.

Why was he suddenly fixated on that human?

"I don't know any—ah, shit. Are you talking about Calamity Keri?"

Luke let out a bark of laughter. "Who?"

"The idiot wolf who can't boil a freaking pot of water without setting off the smoke alarms."

Luke laughed. "*She's* the infamous Keri? Dear goddess, this gets better and better."

"She's *not* my mate."

"Oh, I'm sure she's not." Luke laughed. "But good luck convincing her mother of that."

"How the hell'd you meet her mother?"

Luke gave a huge bearish grin. "She's in the main dining room, having dinner."

Wade groaned. "Please tell me she's alone."

"Nope. She's here with her son and another she-wolf who claims their fourth dinner companion is her daughter, which is weird since the daughter's completely human."

Tessa.

An urgency swept through Wade as his polar bear stretched and let out a deep rumble.

Luke raised an eyebrow. "Your polar's getting a bit agitated there. What's up with that?"

Wade shook his head. "I don't know and I'm too busy to worry about it." He clamped down on his bear and moved down the bar to pull a draft for a waiting customer.

Luke just grinned. "Right. Well, I'll let you get back to it then."

Wade kept as busy as he could throughout the evening, trying to ignore the pull of his polar bear, demanding he go track down Tessa.

There were so many scents in the bar area between

the patrons and the alcohol, he'd had not a single hint she was anywhere in the building until Luke had said something and now he was desperate to track her down.

Then he didn't have to.

Suddenly the two she-wolves were bellied up to the bar, grinning at him.

He sighed and set out napkins for them. "What can I get for you ladies?"

"We still have half a bottle of Witches' Brew right here." Mari set it on the bar in front of them.

Wow.

He didn't sell many bottles of Witches' Brew, mainly because it was so pricey since it also invariably supplied a hell of a lot of alcohol.

Also because very few witches had ever patronized The Ice Box.

So when Luke had placed the order with him earlier, he'd been curious about who had ordered it.

Not once had he suspected these she-wolves, not even after Luke told him they were in the building.

Wade scowled at them. "You didn't let Tessa drink any of this, did you?"

"Of course not," Alexa said. "What kind of mother do you think I am?"

"Yeah," Mari said. "Tessa's been drinking Long Island iced teas all night long."

Wade was horrified. So fine, the Long Island iced tea was

definitely less potent than Witches' Brew, but it was still potent in its own right, especially for humans.

It was also a drink he rarely served at The Ice Box. Mainly because shifters needed a lot more potency to get drunk.

Which meant, if he had to make a guess, the little human had probably been the one to order *all* of the teas he'd made that night, which meant she was probably drunk off her ass.

Before he could demand to know where she was, her scent barreled over him and then she was standing in front of the bar, swaying at Cory's side, eyes glassy, clearly severely impaired.

Cory helped her onto a bar stool, then hopped onto one himself.

"So, Wade," Martha said.

"So I was thinking," Tessa said quickly, making Wade wonder what she thought Martha had been about to say. "I haven't seen a single one of your restaurant kitties, which makes me think you were having me on."

"Eh, it's Zach's day off," Wade said, "and apparently, he took Snowball with him when he left the restaurant yesterday evening."

"Aha! I asked Luke about his kitten and he said he took his home as well. So Luke and Zach both take home *their* kittens, but you don't? I bet you don't even have—"

She broke off as Kahlua and Amaretto raced around the corner of the bar and leapt for her barstool.

Kahlua landed in her lap, making Tessa gasp, before launching forward onto the bar itself.

Amaretto followed his brother, landing and launching from Tessa's lap in seconds.

The she-wolves might be thoroughly drunk, but Wade had to admire their quick reflexes in sweeping their bottle and mugs of Witches' Brew out of the kittens' path.

"Luke only fills in here occasionally," Wade said. "So he's planning to take his kitten to his full-time job at the Worcester Group."

The two kittens barreled to the end of the bar, dropped down onto the countertop behind the bar and raced back toward Wade, weaving their way through all the bottles and bar paraphernalia in their way.

"This would never fly in a human restaurant," Tessa observed.

"Eh, what do shifters care about a bit of fur?" Wade asked.

"Not a lot I would imagine," Tessa said.

"Exactly."

"You know, since Luke is taking his kitten to the Worcester Group, there's a kitten-sized hole here at The Ice Box. I bet Mischief would fit right into that hole."

"Don't even think about it," Wade said.

"But—"

"No."

"You know I hate to agree with Soraya's crazy ideas, but we're on a bit of a time crunch here," Tivali said.

"In what sense?" Bygul asked.

"In the sense that we *do* have other cats to place, *and* other humans to matematch. Not to mention in five days, Tessa goes back to work, at which point she and Wade will be on opposite schedules."

Yeah, that was going to be a bit of a challenge.

"So, if we want them to spend any time together, we need it to happen this week."

"I've got it all under control," Bygul said. "Several things are already in the works."

"Like what?" Tivali demanded. "The vet visit tomorrow? Just because you somehow managed to get Tessa to call the same vet Isana Meier recommended to her brother and cousins doesn't mean they'll actually run into each other there."

"I have to agree," Muezza said, "as the chances of that happening are pretty slim."

"Oh, ye of little faith," Bygul said. "Are we cats of the goddesses or what? A little bit of magical manipulation and miracles can and do happen."

"Personally I vote for Santa Kitty," Soraya said. "*He's* the miracle we need."

Bygul let out a huff of exasperation. "I've got everything under control. There's absolutely no need to call in Kitty Claus."

"Why do you hate him so much?" Soraya demanded.

"Why? Because he's an arrogant, pompous ass.

"The name says it all. His name is Kitty. Not Santa Kitty, just Kitty. That's his name. That's what Mrs. Claus named him. Kitty Claus. But do you think that's enough for him?

"Of course not! He insists that just because he's the cat of the Clauses, he should also be known as Santa Kitty. Give me a break!

"You don't see me walking around calling myself Freyja Bygul, do you? Of course not. That would be ridiculous!

"But he's so arrogant he thinks just because he gets to travel in a sleigh with the Big Man once a year, he's an actual Santa himself. It's outrageous."

"So," Tivali dragged out the word. "What you're basically saying is that you can't stand him because he's a lot like you."

"What? No!"

"You do like to remind people that you're the best matchmaker at PPM," Muezza pointed out.

"I *am* the best!"

Soraya sniffed. "And Santa Kitty is Santa's kitty, so..."

Bygul growled in annoyance. "Fine. Whatever. Call him

in if you must, but I'm telling you now, that crazy cat will just make things worse."

"Yay!" Soraya leapt up and popped out of the room, presumably to track down the idiot Claus.

"Eh, I wouldn't worry about Kitty that much," Muezza said. "Soraya likes to flirt with him and he likes flirting back, so chances are he'll spend most of his time hanging out with her, rather than interfering with our matches."

"Then what's the point of even bothering?" Bygul demanded.

"Because," Tivali said, "he specializes in chaos and as much as we hate to admit it, chaos is typically the turning point for every match."

Bygul growled. He hated that she was right. "You do realize he'll annoy all of us with his arrogant, condescending attitude. He can't help himself."

Tivali just stared at Bygul, a wry look on her face.

Bygul huffed at the incredibly *rude* insinuation that he was *anything* like Kitty Claus.

As if!

Six

"**G**UESS WHO'S FINALLY here?" Soraya cheered as she popped into the room the next morning, Bygul's arch nemesis at her side.

"Oh, great," Bygul muttered. "Idiot Claus is here."

"Yes, yes, happy to help, happy to help," the rotund gray and black feline said as he slowly crossed the room. "Now that the big day is finally behind us, I've got a very small window of time before I have to start gearing up for next year."

Bygul glared at Tivali.

He'd said it, hadn't he? He'd warned her the cat would lord it over them, acting as if he was doing them an incredible favor taking time out of his *busy* and *important* schedule.

The big day.

Whatever.

"So, Bygul," Kitty Claus stretched out on the floor and began to lazily groom himself, licking wherever he could reach, which wasn't far given his girth. "I heard you'd added matematching to your services. Thought it was a joke at first, to be honest. Then I realized you were probably just looking for something to keep you busy. We can't all work for the Clauses, now can we?"

Bygul let out a grunt of annoyance.

The pompous fool was even more arrogant than Bygul remembered, something he would have said was quite impossible even an hour ago.

"So, bad news, Mischief," Tessa said when the kitten woke her that morning. "Well, good news *and* bad news.

"The good news is I never get a hangover, no matter how much I drink. The key is lots of water to flush out your system and a couple ibuprofen before going to bed. Works like a charm every time. So that's good news for me.

"The bad news is that we'll be able to keep our appointment at the vet this afternoon since I'm feeling just fine. I know it's probably not going to be the most exciting thing you've ever done, but I promise, the trip is necessary to ensure you live a long and happy, *healthy* life.

"Plus who knows, maybe you'll make a couple friends while we're there."

Famous last words.

Mischief wasn't sure about the carrier and she definitely did not enjoy the car ride, serenading Tessa the entire way to the vet's office with a series of increasingly strident meows.

However, when Tessa opened the door to the vet's office and a cacophony of dogs barking and cats yowling reached their ears, Mischief went silent.

Tessa got them checked in, then settled on a bench to wait. She set the carrier beside her and leaned down to croon to Mischief inside. "It's okay, baby. Everything's going to be just fine."

At that moment, the outside door opened and Wade Meier walked into the vet's office, carrying a carrier three times the size of Mischief's.

The moment Tessa saw Wade, a wave of heat rushed through her.

The night before, he'd insisted on calling a car service for Alexa and Martha.

When it had arrived, he'd poured them into it, making sure the driver knew exactly where to take them.

Cory had gone off with Luke hours before, so that had just left Tessa.

Given they lived in the same complex, Wade had finished his closing duties at the bar, then had escorted Tessa out to his car.

When they'd arrived at their building, he'd walked her

up the stairs, shoulders brushing, tension building between them.

When they'd reached her door, she'd turned to face him to thank him for the ride, but she hadn't been able to get a word out because he'd pulled her into his arms and kissed her.

Heat had rushed through her in a massive wave, obliterating thought and any inhibitions she might have had.

They'd stood in the hallway outside their apartments, kissing for what seemed like hours before he'd finally nudged her back and into her apartment, where he'd left her with one final, searing kiss.

Memories of that kiss and all the ones that had come before had kept her tossing and turning all night long and had been the first thing she'd thought of this morning when she woke.

Her car was still at The Ice Box, so she'd called a car service to take her to the vet's office.

She hadn't seen Wade when leaving her apartment and had wondered if he would regret their passionate kiss in the light of day.

Now here he was, in the same place at the same time *she* was, without any prior planning or expectation of seeing each other that day.

She was simply blown away at the random vagaries of fate.

Wade approached the front counter, but halfway there, froze and turned his head to glare at Tessa.

She gave a tentative smile and waved.

He shook his head and continued up to the front desk.

A few moments later, he walked over to her bench and plopped down beside her, settling the kennel he carried at their feet.

"What are you doing here?" Tessa asked.

"Vaccinations. You?"

Tessa nodded. "Same."

WADE WAS FLABBERGASTED TO REALIZE TESSA WAS sitting in the waiting room of the vet Isana had recommended.

What were the odds they'd both choose the same vet *and* have appointments at approximately the same time on the same day?

He pondered whether Isana had set him up.

Again.

"How'd you find out about this vet?" he asked suspiciously, wondering if she'd called Isana after all.

"There was a magnet with their phone number on Keri's fridge," Tessa said. "I thought it was odd since as far as I know, she's never had a pet, but it seemed like as good a sign as any."

He grunted, unsure exactly how she'd accomplished it,

but willing to blame Isana for the convenient placement of that magnet.

"Meow."

In response to Mischief's meow, his three started meowing as well.

Tessa leaned over and peeked into Mischief's carrier. "Are you lonely, baby? Want to say hi to the other kitties?"

"Uh, are you sure that's a good idea?" Wade asked nervously as Tessa set her carrier on the floor so it faced his larger one.

"Of course it is. I keep telling you she'd make a terrific—"

Her words were drowned out by a cacophony of hissing, growls and yowls that erupted from both carriers.

"Oh dear." Tessa grabbed her carrier and lifted it up so she could see Mischief. "It's okay, baby. Those mean old kitties aren't going to hurt you."

Wade grunted in exasperation. "You're the one who set her down there. If anyone's traumatized, it's probably my cats."

"Oh, please." Tessa leaned over and peeked into his carrier. "They don't look traumatized to me." She sat back up. "Anyway, back to what we were talking about, I don't suppose you happened to mention a trip to the vet's office to my mom."

Wade gave her an incredulous look.

"Yeah, didn't think so," she muttered. "It just seems rather convenient, don't you think?"

"Why would your mother plant my vet's magnet on your fridge?" It made no sense.

Tessa blushed. "You mean you haven't realized my mother's attempting to matematch us?"

"You mean, you and me?" he exclaimed. "I thought they were trying to match me to Calamity Keri."

"Oh, Martha's definitely convinced you're perfect for Keri." Tessa snickered. "However, I'm pretty sure my mother has her hopes pinned on claiming you for me."

"You do realize it's the height of insanity for those she-wolves to think they can just choose a shifter's fated mate for him?" Wade wasn't sure how much Tessa understood about shifter mates, but he could see by the grin on her face that she did in fact, realize how ridiculous her mother and aunt were being.

"Eh, they're just having some fun. Ever since my uncle Karl passed away, Martha's been obsessed with matematching all the single wolves in the pack."

"But you're not a wolf," Wade said.

"I'm still a pack member and as such, am considered an honorary one."

"How'd that come about? Were you adopted?"

Tessa grinned. "No. My dad met my stepmom when I was nine. Turns out she was the alpha of the local pack. We had no idea shifters existed, of course, so things were fairly intense for a while. Honestly, it felt like a grand adventure at the time. This whole world opened up to me that I'd never known about."

"Tessa Madison," a vet tech called her name.

"Right." Tessa stood and grabbed her carrier. "Catch you later."

A couple minutes later, another vet tech came out and called Wade's name.

He followed the woman into one of the exam rooms and watched as she carefully weighed each cat and got them ready for the visit with the vet.

It was when the tech stepped out of the room that things went to hell.

"Well, that didn't go well," Tivali observed.

"What are you talking about?" Kitty Claus growled. "It was the perfect plan and it's gone off without a hitch."

"You're a menace, K.C." Bygul snapped.

"No, no, no." Kitty Claus said. "That is not my name. I'm Santa Kitty and don't you forget it."

"You're Kitty Claus and that's that," Bygul said. "Santa has nothing to do with it."

K.C. let out a rumbling growl and Bygul gave an answering one back.

"Now, boys," Tivali said. "We have more important things to worry about than Kitty's name. What are we going to do about this situation?" She waved a hand down at the vet's office where chaos had been unleashed.

"Did you have to jolt the kittens so hard?" Muezza asked.

"It worked, didn't it?"

"Except now they're on the hunt for poor Mischief!" Tivali exclaimed.

"Eh, it'll be fine," K.C. said. "Besides, that's what we want, isn't it? Amaretto and Kahlua will hunt down Mischief, with Wade on their tails, and our mission is accomplished."

"How is *that* mission accomplished?" Bygul demanded.

"Because Mischief is with Tessa, which means when Amaretto and Kahlua find them, Wade won't be far behind. In other words, our two targets will get to spend some more time together."

"Yeah, but it won't be quality time," Tivali exclaimed, "especially if they're busy trying to break up a cat fight!"

"I warned you," Bygul said. "I'm pretty sure I said K.C. will just make a bad situation worse."

"Hey!" K.C. exclaimed. "I specialize in chaos. What did you expect?"

TESSA HAD NO IDEA WHAT WAS GOING ON OUTSIDE her exam room.

She could hear the yowls of cats and footsteps running up and down the tile floors, plus the occasional cursing.

"What do you think happened, Mischief? Should we go check it out?"

She leaned over and scooped up the kitten from where she was sniffing all along the crack beneath the exam room door.

A yowl from the opposite side of the door made Tessa jump, then giggle nervously. "What do you think, baby? Did someone's cat escape?"

Making sure she had a good grip on Mischief, Tessa opened the exam room door.

"Mrawr!" Two cats bolted inside the room with hair-raising yowls.

Wade barreled in after them, a third cat in his arms. He slammed the door closed behind him.

"Uh, hi." Tessa grinned. She'd never seen Wade look so frazzled, not that she knew him that well, but he'd always seemed so put together. Now, though, he looked like he'd been through the ringer.

WADE LEANED AGAINST THE COUNTER IN THE EXAM room and tried to catch his breath.

He glared at Amaretto and Kahlua, who had settled in a corner of the room, curling up together and falling asleep. "Seriously? Now, you're all calm?"

The two kittens had raced up and down the hall outside the exam rooms, defying all attempts to catch them while also refusing to go into any of the open exam rooms where they might have been trapped.

But the minute this door opened, they beelined inside and then just settled down like they hadn't been going insane just moments before.

A soft knock came at the door.

Wade reached over and keeping his eyes aimed at the kittens, cracked the door open just enough for the two humans outside to squeeze into the already ridiculously crowded exam room.

"I'm so sorry," the vet said to Tessa. "We can move you to a different exam room if you'd like."

Tessa just grinned. "No, it's fine. Why don't you take care of Mischief here, so we can put her back in her carrier and then you can focus on Wade's little family."

So that's what they did.

The vet tech slipped out to grab Wade's kennel while the vet examined and vaccinated first Mischief, then Bahama Mama, who jumped right into her kennel the minute the examination was over, then Amaretto and finally, Kahlua.

Much to Wade's surprise, when all exams were finished

and vaccinations administered, both Amaretto and Kahlua were happy to join their mother inside their kennel.

"Seriously?" He demanded, hands on hips, glaring in at them.

The vet chuckled. "That's fairly typical. First they refuse to get out of the carrier, then all they want is to return to it. Well, it's been an adventure to say the least. Thanks so much for livening up our work day." She sent them a final grin before slipping out of the room.

A moment later, the vet tech escorted them out to the cashier, where they settled their bills, set up spay/neuter appointments and headed outside.

When they reached the parking lot, Tessa came to a screeching halt. "Damnit."

"What's wrong?"

"My car's still at The Ice Box. I had a service drop us off."

"Come on. I'll give you a ride back to your car. I have to drop the cats off at The Ice Box anyway."

By the time they got to the restaurant, Wade was starving, so he asked Tessa if she'd like to join him for lunch inside.

"Can Mischief come too?"

"Of course, but let's keep her in the carrier. I think one set of escaping cats per day is more than enough."

Tessa raised an eyebrow. "Just how many human neighbors do you have?"

"One as far as I know, but in case you were wondering, I don't go around kissing my shifter neighbors like that either. In fact, since we're on the subject." He leaned over the bar and kissed her.

Heat rushed over Tessa and she tried to get closer, but the bar was in their way.

She clutched his shoulders and lost herself in his kiss.

The sound of a throat clearing broke them apart.

unch is served." The man standing there, who had to be

ed to Wade as he shared the same white-blonde hair and

g build, settled plates on the bar with a grin.

figured this man had to be one of the brothers or the

cause he had a white kitten perched on his

's is my cousin, Zach. Zach, Tessa."

famous Zach who dabbles in conspiracies

nd doorsteps."

the

ight.

oked confused.

"Someone left a kitten outside our

her." He shoved the carrier toward

. Should I?"

d.

n Zach's shoulder onto the

ry human

ed it from one end to the

other before stretching out and hanging her head over the side so she could peer in at Mischief.

Tessa held her breath, then let it out in a whoosh as the white kitten reared back with a hiss and a yowl.

She jumped down in front of the carrier, whirled around and hissed again.

A tiny hiss in response came from inside the carrier.

"Aw, it's okay, Snowball. She's just a tiny kitten, smaller even than you." Zach scooped Snowball into his arms and placed her back on his shoulder. "And don't worry. You're still my best girl. No other kitty could possibly take your place."

Good goddess, that was sweet. What was it about these polar bears and how they handled their cats? So freaking adorable.

At that moment, Mischief slammed her body against the door to the carrier and it popped open.

Before Tessa could grab the kitten, she bolted, hurtling down the bar, leaping for a bar stool. "Mischief, no!" Tessa cried out, lunging to try and catch her, but missing her entirely as the kitten launched for the floor and freedom.

"Mrawr!" Amaretto and Kahlua hurtled from somewhere behind the bar and the chase was on.

"Oh, shit," Wade muttered as the cats hurtled through the restaurant, weaving in and out from under tables and between shifters' feet, leaping from floor to chair to table and back again.

"Ow, Snowball, no!" A white streak launched from Tessa's left and barreled after the other cats.

"This is not good," Zach said, hands on hips.

"THIS IS NOT GOOD," MUEZZA said.

"How did that door pop open like that?" Tivali demanded. "There's no way that kitten had enough strength to make that happen and Tessa was very careful to latch it closed again."

K.C. let out a rumble of amusement. "It's called magic, my dears."

"Why in the world would you use your magic right then?" Bygul demanded. "They were talking, enjoying each other's company, flirting even."

"Eh, the other bear was distracting them. Besides, things were getting a bit boring," K.C. said. "I thought this might liven things up a bit."

"What did I tell you guys?" Bygul demanded. "Did I not say he was going to make things worse? With him on the job, we're doomed."

"Well, on a positive note, they did share that one kiss last night and he kissed her again just now," Soraya said.

"The heat they generated *was* quite promising," Tivali agreed.

Tessa sat at the bar with a drink in front of her and watched as Wade let Bahama Mama and the kittens free from their kennel.

"Meow."

"I know, baby." Tessa lifted Mischief's carrier from the bar stool beside her onto the bar itself. She eased the door open just enough to slip a hand inside to pet Mischief. "I'm sorry I can't set you free, but I'm not sure Amaretto and Kahlua are willing to share their territory with you."

Actually, based on the hissing and growling the instant they'd caught sight of Mischief earlier, she was pretty sure they wouldn't be at all welcoming.

"So what time are we leaving tonight?" Wade asked.

"What?"

"Wednesday night, right?"

Oh, goddess, with everything that had happened at the vet's office, she'd completely forgotten about dinner tonight. "You're really going to come?"

He grinned at her. "That was never in question."

"Uh, I'm pretty sure it was."

"Not since last night."

"What happened—oh. Seriously?"

"Hell, yes. You think I go around kissing my human neighbors like that all the time?"

Tessa raised an eyebrow. "Just how many human neighbors do you have?"

"One as far as I know, but in case you were wondering, I don't go around kissing my shifter neighbors like that either. In fact, since we're on the subject." He leaned over the bar and kissed her.

Heat rushed over Tessa and she tried to get closer, but the bar was in their way.

She clutched his shoulders and lost herself in his kiss.

The sound of a throat clearing broke them apart. "Lunch is served." The man standing there, who had to be related to Wade as he shared the same white-blonde hair and amazing build, settled plates on the bar with a grin.

She figured this man had to be one of the brothers or the cousin because he had a white kitten perched on his shoulder.

"Tessa, this is my cousin, Zach. Zach, Tessa."

"Ah, the infamous Zach who dabbles in conspiracies involving kittens and doorsteps."

"Huh?" Zach looked confused.

Wade chuckled. "Someone left a kitten outside our apartments. Tessa found her." He shoved the carrier toward Zach. "Recognize her?"

Zach peered inside. "No. Should I?"

"It was a theory," Wade said.

The white kitten leapt from Zach's shoulder onto the top of the carrier, where she sniffed it from one end to the

"Yeah, and then the crazy cat went and ruined every-thing," Bygul muttered.

"Santa Kitty's plans are usually quite effective," Soraya said. "You just have to be patient and give the plan time to work."

"Seriously?" Bygul exclaimed.

"She's kind of right," Tivali said. "More often than not, chaos *does* help."

"Are you sure about that?" Bygul demanded."Because Kalyn specializes in chaos as well and I don't remember a single time his brand of chaos was helpful. Well, except for that one time. In *hell*.

"So let's compare. In what universe has *Kitty Claus* ever been effective? And don't say hell,"

Soraya let out a huff. "Well, that's rather limiting, isn't it?"

IT TOOK ALMOST AN HOUR TO CATCH MISCHIEF, who quite enjoyed playing with the other cats' toys, eating their food, rubbing her scent all over their cat beds, racing up and down their climbing trees and using each of their litter boxes.

She was so mischievous.

They'd think they had her trapped and then she'd dart in

some direction they hadn't predicted and the chase would be on again.

She not only led the humans on a very merry chase, but Amaretto, Kahlua and Snowball as well.

They may never have caught her if it weren't for Bahama Mama.

After an hour of exploring the entire restaurant, causing chaos in the office, the pass, the kitchen and even the pastry kitchen, where an orange tabby joined the chase for a while, Mischief finally bolted back toward the bar.

She leapt onto the bar and came face-to-face with Bahama Mama, who lunged and pinned Mischief between her paws and began to groom her.

"Oh my goddess," Tessa gasped, leaning against the bar, trying to catch her breath. "Good job, Mama. Good job."

Wade, Zach and the third Meier, who they introduced as Steve, settled onto bar stools, leaned their backs against the bar and gasped for breath.

"What the hell?" Steve said. "They ruined the mousse. *And* the eclairs."

"Give me a break," Zach panted. "So they don't look as perfect as you planned. They're still quite delicious, I'm sure."

"There are *pawprints* in the mousse. And on the floor." Steve pointed and everyone turned to look.

Sure enough, there was a trail of chocolatey pawprints leading from the bar through the restaurant. "They're all over the pass," Steve said, referring to the long shelf where

dishes were prepped and set out for the wait staff to pick up and deliver, "and they trail from there all the way back to my ruined mousse in the pastry kitchen."

Tessa snickered. "I'm sorry to laugh. I just can't believe none of us could catch her but one second in front of Bahama Mama and she's docile as a lamb."

Wade reached back and scratched Mama on her head. "It's Mama's gift. She's a natural disciplinarian."

"Well, I'd better get back to work," Steve said. "I have replacement desserts to make. Come along, my sweet little Eclair." He picked up the orange tabby who was lounging on the floor at his feet, draped her over one shoulder and headed back toward the kitchen.

"Me too," Zach said, "but don't worry. I'll check back in regularly, make sure you guys don't need anything else."

"Oh, that's not necessary," Tessa said.

Zach grinned. "Of course it is, my dear. It's necessary because I enjoy torturing my cousin." He leaned over and planted a kiss on Tessa's cheek.

Wade lunged and Zach leapt back with a laugh. "Maybe put Mischief back into her carrier. You know, before she escapes again."

Tessa whirled and saw that Mama Bahama had apparently lost interest in grooming the kitten and was now grooming herself.

As a result, Mischief was in the process of slinking away.

Tessa quickly scooped her up and cuddled her close. "I hate to put her back in that tiny carrier."

"Here." Wade walked around the bar, then carried his much larger carrier around to set it on the floor. "She can hang out in there until we're ready to head out. Now let's eat." He eyed their lunches that had been sitting on the bar, untouched for more than an hour. "Maybe I should order us replacement meals."

"Don't be ridiculous. Even cold, a meal from The Ice Box is probably delicious." Tessa leaned over, opened the larger carrier and placed Mischief inside. "Wow. You have a litter box *and* a cat bed in there."

"There's no reason for them to be uncomfortable while traveling, now is there?"

Tessa shook her head, speechless once again at how well this bear cared for his cats.

THE REST OF THE AFTERNOON PASSED QUICKLY AS they ate lunch together and talked.

Of course, Zach kept his promise to stop by periodically and torture Wade.

He was getting really good at that.

"I'm so glad to discover that Wade actually has friends outside this bar," Zach said on one of his many annoying visits. "I was starting to worry that he has no life."

Wade growled, annoyed at Zach's obnoxious flirting, especially since he already had his own mate.

Wade glared across the restaurant toward their hostess, Lumiki, but she simply grinned back at him.

Why wasn't she dragging Zach away to stake her claim? Couldn't she see her mate was standing entirely too close to Wade's?

Wait a minute.

Did he just refer to Tessa as his mate?

Wade was so shocked, he almost missed what Zach said next.

"I mean look at him. He actually thinks his place of employment—on his day off, no less—is the perfect setting for a date."

Tessa grinned. "It's worse than that."

"How could it possibly be worse?"

"It's our *first* date."

"No way!" Zach exclaimed.

Wade let out a growl. "It is *not* our first date. We were here last night too."

"I was with my mother, my aunt and my cousin," Tessa said. "You cannot possibly consider last night our first date."

"Did we not kiss at the end of it?"

Tessa blushed, then glared at him.

He just grinned back unrepentantly.

"I'd like to point out that if yesterday *does* count as your first date," Zach said, "that means Wade thinks his place of employment is an excellent setting not only for a first date, but for the second one as well."

Tessa burst into laughter.

Wade growled. "You're not helping, Zach. Go away."

"Wait. Was I *supposed* to be helping?"

IF IT HADN'T BEEN FOR POOR MISCHIEF, WHO definitely needed her freedom from the carrier, Tessa probably would have stayed at The Ice Box with Wade until it was time to head for Martha's house that evening.

As it was, she stayed much longer than planned, though she had to admit, she had a great time.

"I really like your brothers and cousin," she said to Wade as he walked her to her car.

He scowled. "But not more than you like me, right?"

She grinned up at him. "Well, none of them have made me go weak in the knees, so probably not."

"Probably, huh?" They reached her car and after unlocking the doors, he settled the smaller empty carrier and the larger one holding Mischief onto the backseat.

He then closed the door, leaned against it and pulled her close. "I think we need to work on making that a definitely."

He then proceeded to kiss her until all her thoughts were

scrambled, she was rubbing against him like a cat in heat and clutching at his shoulders, trying desperately to get closer.

Long, drugging moments later, he pulled away, opened her driver's side door and settled her inside. He then sent her off with one final, searing kiss and a promise to pick her up at six-thirty to journey to Martha's for dinner.

Seven

TESSA WOKE THE next morning smiling at her memories of dinner at Martha's the night before.

She giggled picturing the look on Wade's face when he'd emerged from the guest bathroom to whisper in her ear, "The ugliest creature on earth just stared at me while I was peeing."

She'd burst into laughter and had then shared with everyone Wade's opinion of Martha's recent bathroom acquisitions.

Of course, this set off a steady flow to the bathroom, where everyone had to share their opinions upon emerging.

The general consensus was ugly, not cute.

Martha kept insisting that they were so ugly, that *made* them cute, but no one else seemed to agree.

Not even Cory would take her side on that one.

"They're hideous, Mom," he announced upon emerging

from the bathroom. "Absolutely hideous. If you paid more than a penny for both, you got robbed."

Martha gasped while everyone else roared with laughter.

It had been a truly wonderful night.

Wade had fit right in or at least he *had* until Martha finally got a clue and realized her niece had stolen her daughter's intended mate.

"I cannot believe you would do that to Keri," Martha had wailed.

Tessa had simply rolled her eyes. "Give me a break. Keri was never going to mate Wade."

"You don't know that," Martha said. "Now that you've stolen him, I suppose she won't, but she might have if you hadn't interfered."

"Oh, give it up, Martha," Alexa said with a laugh. "Just accept that you're not that good at matematching."

Martha let out a gasp that ruffled her hair. "I beg your pardon."

"It was pretty obvious from minute one that he was meant for *my* daughter, not yours."

"So it's a conspiracy," Martha exclaimed. "You two were working together to steal my daughter's mate and my grandbabies right out from under me."

Wade snickered. "Is she always this dramatic?" He muttered in Tessa's ear.

"Always."

"Please tell me she's not going to hold this against you."

Tessa giggled. "Of course not. She'll be over it by

tomorrow and by Friday, she'll be taking credit for every-thing. Goddess forbid I end up your mate because she'll never let us live it down. She'll claim credit for every moment of our relationship, including every child we have from the union. You should definitely run away as fast as you can."

He'd let out a bark of laughter. "Yeah, that's not happen-ing. The she-wolf is scary, but not as scary as walking away from you."

Tessa got ready for the day, holding close the memory of those words and of the heated kisses he'd given her at the end of the night.

WADE WOKE THE MORNING AFTER SPENDING THE evening with Tessa and her family, determined to claim his mate.

First though, he needed to court her.

He'd pinned her down about her schedule the night before.

It turned out his Tessa was a second grade teacher and her cousin, Cory, taught fifth grade.

They worked at the same elementary school and were both on break until the following Tuesday.

Knowing they had very limited time before their work schedules would limit that time even further, they'd made plans to see each other every day until she went back to work.

Today, he was taking her to the aquarium in Worcester Falls. She'd apparently never been before.

"Wait, it's a Shenanigans too?" Tessa exclaimed when they arrived, staring up at the aquarium's huge sign. 'What is up with that brand name?"

"It tells paranormals this is a safe place for them. No humans get past the magical barriers unless they're with a paranormal. This particular Shenanigans is run by a slew of paranormals interested in conservation and wildlife. Shifters, witches, chameleons. Even the gods and goddesses sometimes get involved. Hell, the demons and demonesses do as well. We all share the same world and it's in our best interests to save it."

"I love that," Tessa said. "Even though I've been immersed in the shifter world for a couple decades now, I still find myself learning new things all the time, but I think this is the best so far."

TESSA STARED AROUND AT THE AQUARIUM complex, trying to take it all in. The map they'd been given showed the complex sprawled over an enormous amount of land, consisting of huge buildings and arenas that showcased both outdoor and indoor aquariums, and would probably take days to walk in its entirety.

They chose a building at random and as they walked through it, Tessa was overwhelmed at the information provided about the marine life they visited and the ongoing conservation efforts to save them.

"This is amazing," Tessa breathed as they stood in a tunnel and stared up at the underside of huge sharks and colorful fish and other marine life.

She was riveted, unable to look away.

Wade hooked an arm around her waist, tugged her into a small alcove between two aquariums and kissed her. He plunged his tongue deep and all thoughts of marine life were obliterated as Tessa clutched his shoulders and kissed him back.

Long moments later, they finally separated, both of them breathing heavily.

"What was that?" Tessa gasped. "One minute I'm staring at sharks and the next—whew."

He grinned. "I couldn't take it. The look on your face, how immersed you were in the whole experience." He shook his head. "I needed your attention back on me."

Tessa grinned. "Well, you definitely got that. Feel free to do it again, anytime."

He let out a sexy rumble that made her shiver in anticipation. "You can count on it."

The rest of the day was magical. Between the marine and fresh water wildlife they visited, all the things she learned during those visits and the many, many devastating kisses Wade delivered between practically every single exhibit, Tessa was a mass of exposed nerves and aching needs by the time they left the aquarium that evening.

They'd had lunch in the cafeteria and had spent a good hour feeding each other and talking about everything and nothing and of course, punctuating almost every bite with a kiss.

By the time they left the aquarium around six that evening, though, their lunch had long since worn off.

Wade took her to a Shenanigans restaurant that wasn't The Ice Box, but that served food that was just as wonderfully delicious.

They spent hours talking and eating and driving their needs higher.

By the time they got back to the apartment complex, Tessa was one giant ball of need.

They walked up the stairs, much the way they had the two previous nights, shoulders brushing, tension mounting, desperation in the air.

This time when they reached their floor, Wade took Tessa's hand in his and led her to his apartment door.

He unlocked the door, pulled her inside, kicked the door shut and backed her up against the opposite wall.

She flung her arms around his neck, he hitched her up and she hooked her legs around his waist.

He braced her against the wall and took her mouth with his, plunging his tongue deep.

Tessa writhed against him, shoving her hands between them so that she could drag his shirt free of his jeans.

She dragged it up and leaned back enough so that she could whip it over his head.

She pulled his head down and kissed him again, tongues rubbing against each other, breath mingling, desperation in every movement.

Wade shoved her shirt upward, dragged it off, then went to work on her bra.

She hitched herself up and forward so that he could reach the hooks in the back. He managed to get it unhooked and her bra straps fell forward.

He shoved the bra away and closed his hands over her breasts.

She whimpered and writhed against him. "Wade."

He straightened, tightened his arms around her and walked them down the hall past the living room and kitchen into the back hallway that led to the bedrooms.

He tossed her onto his bed and she bounced a little, then went to work on her jeans, dragging them free, unable to take her eyes from him as he did the same.

She licked her lips as his cock sprang free.

Before she could spend too much time admiring it, though, he moved and was suddenly directly over her, cock nudging her entrance.

He leaned down and kissed her, one hand stroking her breast while the other reached down to guide him home.

"Wade."

"Aw, goddess, Tessa, my love." He entered her slowly, giving her time to adjust to his girth, pausing, then surging forward again until finally he was rooted deep.

Still kissing her, he slowly pulled away, then moved forward again.

She wrapped her legs around his waist and surged up to meet him.

He braced a hand on the bed beside her and hooked the opposite arm beneath her knee, lifting her leg high, sinking even deeper with that one action.

"Wade!" Tessa gasped.

He pulled back then surged forward again, rubbing something deep inside that made everything in her coil tighter and tighter.

She cried out as he plunged over that same spot again and again until heat exploded through her, erasing the world in a million fractures of light.

"What did I say?" K.C.'s voice was annoyingly smug. "Letting the kitten out of the carrier was definitely the right move."

"That happened yesterday and has nothing to do with them finally getting together today," Bygul said in exasperation. "In fact, if they hadn't been so exhausted from chasing all those cats all over the restaurant, we might have arrived at this ending yesterday!"

"You sure are grumpy for having a match go so well for once," K.C. said. "It's a good thing you invited me, Soraya. Who knows what would have happened to this match without my intervention?"

Tivali snorted.

Bygul was pretty sure she was seconds away from laughing.

At his pain!

"I told you he'd be like this," Bygul growled. "He's insufferable and it's no thanks to him this match is finally on track."

"I don't disagree," Tivali said, "but as long as he's gloating, he's not actually interfering."

That was a good point. "Fine. I'll let him rest on his stolen laurels while we get back to the hard work. You know, it really was quite genius to place that pamphlet to the aquarium in the cat carrier."

"It was Muezza's idea," Tivali said.

"Well, excellent team work planting it there so he'd think she wanted to go and arrange it for her," Bygul said. "You could literally see them falling in love as they wandered through the many buildings."

"I know," Tivali said. "Soraya kept going on and on about how romantic it was, the way Wade couldn't take his eyes off her and how she kept their hands laced together the entire time."

"Pretty sure Soraya was hinting at K.C. with all that sighing," Muezza said.

Tivali snorted. "She's been rolling around in the catnip a bit too much if she thinks that cat's ever going to settle down. Word has it he's a big flirt with no follow-through."

"Okay, that is way more information than we needed," Bygul said.

"Agreed," Muezza said.

THE NEXT DAY WAS LIKE A DREAM FOR TESSA. THEY spent the entire day indulging their passion, then went out that evening with Cory and Luke.

"I have to warn you," Tessa said, "Cory and I have standing Friday night plans that usually involve dinner somewhere in Pleasantville since that's where we work, then drinks at a Shenanigans gay bar.

"Sounds like fun," Wade said with a grin. "Far be it for me to disrupt your plans. I assume it's okay for me to tag along?"

"Of course. Apparently Luke is joining us as well, so this will be a whole new type of outing for us."

And it was.

They had so much fun at dinner.

Though the brothers had occasionally eaten at human

establishments ("usually when there are no other choices around," Luke explained), they'd never been to a Cracker Barrel before.

"I don't get it," Wade said as he gazed around the racks of clothing and knickknacks on shelves. "I thought this was a restaurant."

Tessa giggled. "It is. We've just gotta get through the impulse shopping portion of the experience." She dragged him through the racks to the hostess stand, where they put in their name and waited to be seated.

"I still don't get it," Wade said. "Do humans actually shop here? I mean I guess I can see the appeal of the rocking chairs, but why would you come here for clothes or candles or whatever all is out there."

"Oh, people don't come here to shop," Tessa said. "They come here to eat and then they buy things they don't need because they have no self-control."

Cory snickered.

"I mean I'm sure there's someone out there who's come to the Cracker Barrel just to buy and not to eat, but I'd be willing to bet most people who come to buy, end up staying to eat as well, so basically, this place is like a black hole where good intentions come to die."

Wade, Luke and Cory laughed.

"So, why do you guys come here again?" Wade asked.

"It's an experience and it's close to our school," Cory said.

"But you guys didn't work today, so why not go some-where else tonight?"

"Because it's an experience," Cory and Tessa chorused.

"And we wanted to share that experience with you guys," Tessa continued.

We're honored," Luke said dryly.

Wade just grinned.

The food was excellent, of course, though perhaps not quite as good or as plentiful as the food at a Shenanigans restaurant, but still enjoyable.

They left the restaurant laughing and drove to Worcester Falls, to a gay bar Luke recommended.

Upon arrival, Tessa announced it was her turn to be designated driver, to which Cory pumped a fist in joy before they all walked into the bar together.

Tessa had a fabulous time, as she usually did, watching Cory burn up the dance floor. It turned out Luke was quite the dancer as well so the two of them together were on fire.

"Wow," Wade said in her ear. "I've literally never seen Luke tear up the dance floor like that."

"Seriously?"

"Well, I mean, it's not like we go dancing together and I had no idea he could dance like that. Damn. I'm going to have to take some pictures—a *lot* of pictures—and share them with the entire family."

"You're terrible," Tessa giggled.

By the end of the night, Tessa was completely charmed by how relaxed Wade was in a gay bar and how unbothered

he was by the fact that men kept hitting on him all night long.

She ended up quizzing Wade on what class of paranormal each man was, and as it turned out, Wade was considered hot not just by humans or shifters, but also by witches, chameleons, and even a trans demoness.

They stayed until last call, then stumbled out into the parking lot so Tessa could drive everyone home. She dropped Cory and Luke off at Cory's place, then drove home, where they stopped at her apartment to scoop up Mischief and a few supplies, then retired to Wade's place.

She'd felt terrible when she remembered she'd left Mischief all alone the night before and had sneaked across the hall at three in the morning to move her into Wade's apartment.

She'd moved Mischief back to her own apartment right before they left to meet up with Cory and Luke, but now she wanted her with them again.

"We're going to need to get more cat supplies," Tessa said, "I'm definitely not enjoying hauling litter boxes and food bowls back and forth."

"Tomorrow," Wade said as he set down the food bowls in his kitchen, hooked an arm around Tessa's shoulders and walked her back toward his bedroom.

The hours that followed were as hot and steamy as the night before.

"That's a good sign," Muezza said.

"It's an excellent sign," Bygul said. "I predict in another day or two, she'll be moving across the hall permanently and they'll have doubled up on supplies for no reason at all."

"Don't you think we should give them another push?" K.C. asked.

"No!" Tivali, Muezza, Soraya and Bygul all shouted.

"We could make a pipe burst, get them all wet. That might speed things along."

"Things are already speeding along," Bygul said. "Did you even notice they went to bed together? If you burst a pipe, you'll puncture the mood as well."

"Maybe we could set a fire. That should heat things up."

"No!" Tivali, Muezza, Soraya and Bygul shouted again.

"Just stop trying to help, okay?" Bygul demanded. "The romance is progressing nicely and they don't need any help from us. At this point, it's all but a done deal."

"Well, fine," K.C. said. "I was just trying to help, but since you clearly don't appreciate the expertise I bring to the table, I'll be on my way." He slowly lumbered to his feet, then stood for a few moments as if waiting for them to protest his decision.

No one said a word, not even Soraya.

"Well, it's been fun, team. I'm so happy I was able to

help get this match back on track. Wishing you the best of luck in the future, especially if you ever decide to take on a more challenging population. Personally, if you're looking for a bit more of a challenge, I recommend the witches."

With that, he popped away, a trail of laughter streaming in his wake.

"Thank the goddess," Soraya said, shocking Bygul. "I thought he'd never leave."

"Wait. You were the one who wanted us to invite him," Bygul exclaimed.

"I don't know what I was thinking," Soraya said. "Supposedly he's this amazing matematcher, but in reality, he's a total mess, kind of like his personality."

"Pretty sure I warned you of that very thing," Bygul said.

"Yes, yes, I know. You were right. Some things, though, we just have to learn for ourselves."

Huh. That was surprisingly perceptive for Soraya.

Eight

NEW YEAR'S EVE dawned bright and early.

Unfortunately, though Wade had convinced Zach to cover his shift the night before, there was no one who could cover for New Year's Eve.

That was because they had their annual New Year's Eve celebration at The Ice Box that evening. It was a huge event everyone they knew was invited to.

In order to be ready in time for everyone to start arriving around seven that evening, Wade went in at ten that morning.

He left Tessa snuggled in bed with Mischief, giving her a kiss and extracting her promise to stop by later that afternoon to have lunch with him.

He then spent the entire day running around the restau-

rant and bar like a madman trying to inventory all their alcohol and get ready for the biggest party of the year.

Tessa joined him for lunch, then went out with her mother and aunt, to shop for a New Year's Eve dress.

"Didn't you leave it rather last minute?" he asked.

"Yes, but I didn't have plans until very last minute."

He scowled. "You mean you weren't going to do anything to celebrate New Year's Eve?"

She shrugged. "I never have in the past. It just didn't seem worth it to be out on the streets with drunken idiots. I always prefer to stay in my pajamas, drink alcohol in the comfort of my own home and go to bed at a decent hour."

He rolled his eyes. "That's very antisocial of you."

"Well, this year, I have a boyfriend, so I'll be celebrating with him."

"Uh, no," he said.

"No?"

"No. You do not have a boyfriend. You have a mate and you will be celebrating with me."

Her face lit up with pure joy. "Are you serious? You really think I'm your mate?"

He leaned over the bar, pulled her halfway onto it and kissed her. "I thought you realized. My bear's terribly grumpy whenever you're not around. For that matter, so am I. So yes, you're most definitely my mate."

BYGUL, TIVALI, SORAYA AND MUEZZA WERE celebrating with tuna and catnip when Kitty Claus popped into the room.

Bygul growled at the unexpected intrusion and launched himself at K.C.

The two cats tumbled across the floor.

It wasn't a great match because Kitty Claus was so huge, he could probably squash Bygul flat, but he also moved so slowly, Bygul easily pinned him. "Why are you back?"

"Thought I'd join the celebration, though I don't know why you bother. After all, the bear would have found his fated mate with or without your assistance. That's the way it works for shifters."

"That's not true," Soraya said hotly.

"Bears are notoriously difficult," Bygul said, climbing off K.C. and turning his back on him. He swished his tail in warning and sauntered away.

"Exactly," Tivali said, "and since Tessa is human, without our help, Wade may never have figured out she was his mate."

"You mean without *my* help," K.C. said.

"You are so annoying, I cannot even," Bygul said. "Why are you here?"

"I just heard about a newly formed coven of witches.

They're in dire need of both familiars *and* mates so I thought I'd bring them to your attention, just in case you're looking for a challenge."

THE ICE BOX HAD LINES OUTSIDE IT SNAKING IN every direction.

"I can't believe I let you drag me to this." A woman behind Tessa complained to the man beside her. "What kind of mate are you anyway, dragging me to something you know I'll hate?"

"Now, Maggie, we don't have to stay long, but we should at least put in an appearance. Isana promised there would be an office you can escape to anytime you want. And bonus, there are cats in the office."

"Really?"

"Yep. Word has it there are at least four kittens and a mama cat hanging there tonight."

"Well, that doesn't sound so bad. I'll just plan to stay in there for most of the night. That works for me."

The other woman standing with them chuckled, drawing Tessa's attention, which was when she realized the two men standing side-by-side were absolutely identical.

"Just don't mention the cats to Mason," the woman said, "or he'll hide in there with you all night long."

The man standing at her side let out a bark of laughter. "Considering he's mated to Isana, I'm guessing Mason already knows about the cats and has his own plans for slipping away to play with them."

"Yeah, you're probably right. Sorry, Maggie, sounds like you may have to put up with Mason if you want to play with the cats."

Maggie shrugged. "That's fine. I like your brother, Kate. He always says exactly what he means and he likes animals, so I can tolerate him better than I can most other people."

"You'd be the first," the man standing next to Kate muttered.

At that moment, the doors to The Ice Box opened and the crowds outside slowly began winding their way through the maze of rope barriers leading to the doors of the restaurant.

"This is going to be epic," Cory exclaimed at her side as they slowly moved forward. Practically the entire pack was at their back.

The invitations had been addressed to *Tessa and Family* and to *Cory and Family*.

Tessa had tried to explain to both Wade and Luke that the concept of family in a wolf pack was very broad.

They'd just laughed and said everyone was welcome.

Tessa really hoped that was the case because there had to be at least thirty members of the pack planning to attend under the umbrella of family.

They'd almost reached the doors when Cory exclaimed, "Hey, Nick, Ryan, how's it going?"

Tessa's eyes widened when she saw another group of wolves from a neighboring pack, who'd apparently been in one of the lines snaking in from the opposite direction, and who were now converging on the door at the same time as them.

"Hey, Cory, Tessa," Nick grinned. "How'd you guys rate the invitation of the year?"

"We found our mates this past week," Luke said. "And they're both Meiers."

"No way," Ryan exclaimed. "What are the chances?"

"So which Meier?" Nick asked.

"I'm with Luke and Tessa's with Wade."

"Oh, man," Ryan said. "They are both delish."

"No kidding," Nick said. "You two hit the jackpot."

"So are you guys somehow related as well?"

"It's convoluted," Nick said. "Basically we're connected to the Worcesters, who are connected to the Meiers. Hey, Jefferson."

"Hey, guys." It was one of the twins standing behind them.

"This is starting to feel very nepotistic," Tessa said, causing everyone around them to laugh.

"That's pretty much every New Year's Eve party at The Ice Box," a woman standing at the door said. "Welcome to The Ice Box, where everyone is a friend."

When they stepped inside, Tessa was amazed.

The entire restaurant had been transformed.

Each of the vast dining rooms had been cleared out. All the tables and chairs were gone. The only furniture in any of the rooms were long tables set against the walls, covered in delicious-looking finger foods, and the barstools at the bar.

"Standing room only," Cory murmured in Tessa's ear.

This was definitely not Tessa's scene.

There were huge disco balls hanging from the ceilings, strobe lights were going crazy and the music was loud and intense.

It was like the busiest clubs Keri and Cory had dragged her to in college times a million.

There were entirely too many people and she was starting to think she might have to escape the crowds by joining Maggie and this unknown Mason in the office to play with the cats.

Cory snorted.

"What?"

"I know exactly what you're thinking and you're not escaping until we've found your mate."

"Then let's get looking. Chances are, he'll be at the bar." She snagged Cory's arm and started across the restaurant. "Once we find him, we can send him after Luke."

They reached the bar and immediately claimed two bar stools.

Tessa let out a breath of relief at getting away from the crowds. "I'm shocked these hadn't been claimed yet. It's already so crowded in here."

"Eh, people are too busy socializing."

"Well, feel free. If Wade doesn't show up soon, I'm going to be helping myself to some of the alcohol behind the bar."

A few moments later, Wade swept toward them, a giant box of liquor in his arms and a huge grin on his face.

He set the box on the bar, lifted Tessa right off her stool into his arms and devoured her mouth in a kiss that sent her up in flames.

Luke arrived a moment later and swept Cory into his arms in a move reminiscent of Wade's.

Tessa grinned. "You sure can tell you guys are brothers."

"Yeah? Well, as long as I'm the only brother you're kissing, I'm okay with that." As if just mentioning it meant he had to do it, Wade kissed her again.

The rest of the night was much the same.

People came and went from the bar area, where Wade and three other bartenders were run ragged trying to meet all the alcohol requests.

The next time Wade had to run to replenish inventory, he dragged Tessa with him, which meant their inventory break took a bit longer than perhaps was warranted, what with all the kissing and groping.

The night continued in much the same vein, with Tessa hanging out at the bar, keeping Wade company and drinking an endless supply of Long Island Iced Teas interspersed with bottles of water.

The rest of the Meiers came by to introduce themselves,

so Tessa ended up meeting Isana Meier and her mate, who turned out to be the infamous Mason.

"So I hear you like cats," Tessa said to Mason, whose face lit up at the question.

He immediately whipped out his phone and started sharing with her pictures of all of his cats, including a giant tomcat named Reaper and three teenage cats named Catphrodite, Furcules and Purrseidon.

Isana rolled her eyes and warned Tessa she might have just doomed herself to cat conversations and cat photos with Mason at every family event until the end of time.

Tessa didn't think that sounded too bad so she just laughed and waved a hand in acknowledgement.

Zach stopped by periodically to tease Wade, wondering out loud if he'd managed to figure out whether Tessa was his mate or not.

Wade informed him that he had and she was.

Tessa simply beamed in joy at the public declaration.

Luke swung by to find out whether Wade had succumbed to the she-wolves and mated Calamity Keri. He winked at Tessa while asking the question, so she knew he was just messing with Wade, who roared in rage and threatened Luke with bodily dismemberment if he ever implied anyone other than Tessa was his mate again.

Luke laughed uproariously, planted a kiss on Tessa's cheek with a heartfelt, "Congratulations, darling," and darted away before Wade managed to get around the bar and throw him as he threatened.

Even Steve, who Tessa understood was fairly antisocial, stopped by to drop off a specially prepared dessert plate just for Tessa, along with his congratulations.

The desserts were so beautifully plated, with various strands of syrups winding around them that Tessa took several picture to commemorate the moment. She thanked Steve profusely and watched in amazement as he blushed, then tried one of the desserts and almost had an orgasm on the spot.

"Oh, my goddess," she groaned around the exquisite bite-size dessert that practically melted in her mouth. "What is this? It's *orgasmic*."

"It's my own recipe," Steve said. "Haven't named it yet."

"Orgasm on a plate. There's your name."

The next thing Tessa knew, Wade had hold of the plate and her arm and was ushering her away from the bar, down the hall toward the offices, where they discovered Maggie and Mason playing with the kittens.

"Dammit," Wade muttered. "Come on." He dragged her further down the hall, then pulled her into the janitorial closet.

"Really?"

"Oh, yeah. Time for another dessert, baby."

Standing there, surrounded by brooms, mops and cleaning supplies, Wade slowly hand-fed Tessa bite-sized desserts in between long and devastating kisses.

By the time they returned to the bar, it was minutes before the countdown.

"Tessa! Tessa!" Cory broke through the crowds and shoved his phone in Tessa's face. "Here. Talk to Keri."

"Oh, my goddess, Keri, you look fantastic. How's the vacation? Where in the world are you?"

"Oh, you know, everywhere and nowhere."

"Well, you're missing the most amazing party."

"Yeah, well, it sounds like I'm missing out on more than that," Keri said. "What's this I hear about you stealing my mate?"

Tessa groaned. "How'd you find out about that?"

"I have my ways." Keri laughed. "Better you than me is all I have to say. That is one grumpy polar bear."

Wade popped his head into the frame, nudging Tessa a little to the side so their faces were cheek to cheek on the camera. "Hey, Calamity Keri." Despite the words he spoke, there was true affection in his voice.

Keri grinned. "Hey, Wade. Didn't I always say there was the right person out there for you? I had no idea it'd be my favorite cousin, but I definitely like fate's sense of humor."

"You and me both," he rumbled, dropping a kiss on Tessa's head. "Come on baby, we're about to start the countdown."

"Okay. Catch you later, Keri. Happy New Year!"

"Happy New Year!"

Tessa passed the phone back to Cory, who wished his sister a happy new year as well, then turned to face Luke just as the countdown began.

Tessa grinned at Wade as all around them, people shouted, "10—9—8"

He pulled her close and started giving her short, sweet kisses in time to the shouts. When they reached one, the kiss was neither short nor sweet.

He plundered her mouth, making her breath catch and heat spread in waves from the top of her scalp to the bottoms of her feet.

Tessa kissed him back with just as much heat and passion as everyone around them shouted, "Happy New Year!"

HER HUMANS HAD COME HOME QUITE LATE THAT evening.

Mischief had let them know she didn't appreciate their tardiness.

Of course, they'd given her much attention and appropriate stroking and loving words had commenced.

Now, her humans were sound asleep and Mischief was bouncing around the apartment, thrilled to have her two humans in the same place with her.

She'd go sleep with them soon, but first she had things to do.

Like attack Wade's sock-monster.

Rahr! She leapt and rolled across the floor with his giant sock. It smelled like him.

She liked it so she dragged it to one of the cat beds, the one she liked the most because it was so soft and warm.

She shoved the sock into her bed and then spent hours kneading that sock into the tiny crevasse along the edges.

Finally, the sock was perfectly positioned.

She gave it a couple more sniffs, then bounded down the hall.

Along the way, she sniffed at everything the humans had dropped on their way to the bedroom when they'd first arrived home.

Shoes.

More shoes.

Another one of Wade's socks.

Mischief pondered that sock for a moment. It smelled like him too, but maybe she should leave that one for him. After all, she knew how to share.

She took one and left one for him, which she considered to be exceptionally generous.

She moved on.

Pants.

Boxers. She rolled around in them for a couple minutes because they smelled like Wade too.

Dress.

Underwear.

Those smelled like Tessa and she didn't have anything that smelled like Tessa yet so Mischief dragged those panties all the way down the hall to her favorite bed where she'd stored Wade's sock.

She dragged the underwear into the bed and started kneading it into position too.

Perfect!

She whirled and raced back down the hall, pausing to sniff at Tessa's bra, which also smelled like her, but Mischief was all about fair.

She only took one sock of Wade's, so she'd only take one piece of underwear from Tessa.

Besides, she could always get more tomorrow.

Mischief bounded up onto the bed and wriggled her way in between her two humans.

She settled down so that her nose was buried in Tessa's ear and her tail was wrapped around Wade's neck.

It was a truly perfect homecoming.

Read on for an excerpt from HOCUS PURRCUS.

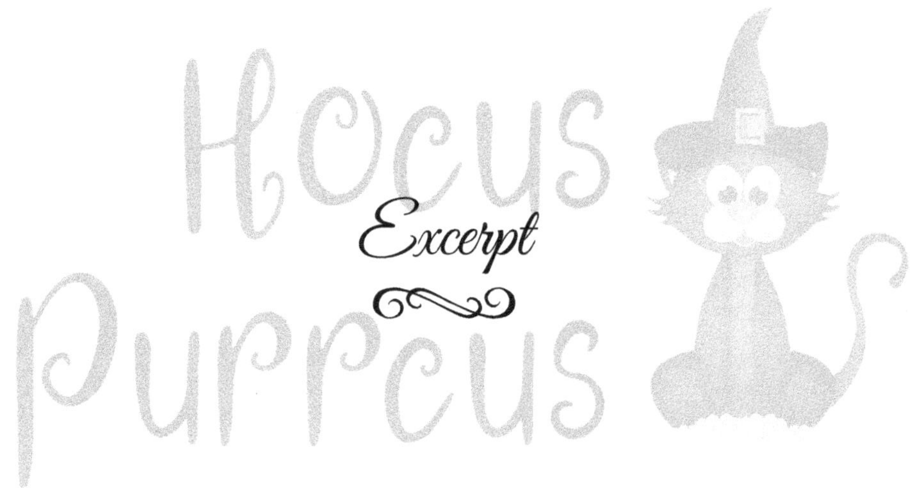

Bygul blamed Kitty Claus for this latest assignment.

Ever since K.C. mentioned how *challenging* witches were to work with, it was all the other matchmaking cats could talk about.

Even though they already had full case loads, the cats were determined to move witches to the top of their list.

Then K.C. returned to tell them of a newly formed coven in need of both familiars and mates.

That was when Bygul knew all his protests would come to naught.

As far as the other cats were concerned, this coven represented a pawsitively purrfect opportunity to match a lot of homeless cats with their purrfect human companions *and* to do some matematching as well.

At least that's what Soraya kept saying, and unfortunately, Tivali and Muezza agreed with her.

Which meant Bygul was along for the ride, because there was absolutely no way he could trust those three to matematch a bunch of witches without his assistance.

The moment they arrived in the tiny town of Zero, though, and Bygul saw exactly who the members of the coven were, and even worse, who its leader was, he knew K.C. had set them up.

The lazy, pompous cat was probably laughing his fool head off right now.

Because there was no way even the best matchmaker at Pawsitively Purrfect Matches—Bygul himself, thank you very much—could help these insane witches achieve their happily ever afters.

Pippa was bored.

Not a good circumstance, to be sure, but it couldn't be helped.

In the beginning, she'd been thrilled to find other witches in similar circumstances as her own—that is to say, lone witches without a coven to anchor their magic—and had leapt at the opportunity to form a coven with these slightly unstable—okay, mostly unstable—witches.

In the beginning, it had been wonderful.

They'd settled in this small town called Zero, which in

Pippa's opinion had been on a downward slide toward a population count that matched its name, when they had arrived.

A somewhat charming, sleepy town in the middle of nowhere, Kansas, where any magic Pippa's newly formed coven happened to unleash would be mostly unseen by the rest of the world.

In fact, it was the perfect spot for the brand of chaos that Pippa's magic tended to cause.

It was wonderful in the beginning.

Not having to worry about her coven members judging her for her lack of control over her magic.

It wasn't her fault that the well from which her magic sprang was more like an ocean with hurricane-force winds, now was it?

Yet, her original coven—The Witches of Salem, dating back to 1600, thank you very much (so very pompous and cliched, not to mention, wrong)—had believed exactly that.

Pippa was a danger to society, they claimed, and too bad it was the twenty-first century, for if she'd been born back at the formation of Salem, she'd have been burned at the stake for certain, and the world spared her out-of-control magic.

While that might have been true, Pippa couldn't believe they'd found it necessary to point it out. Rude!

Then they'd given her a choice—be stripped of her magic or banished.

Well, no one was stealing Pippa's power, even if it did make her life chaotic and miserable upon occasion.

So Pippa had chosen the lone witch lifestyle, which wasn't much different than the rest of her life, given her parents had died when she was a child and the rest of the coven had washed their hands of her long before her banishment.

It was the glitter incident that had been the final straw.

It wasn't as if she'd done it on purpose. She'd been trying to multiply the pastries for the meeting that afternoon and well, she'd ended up casting the vacuum cleaner instead, not that she'd realized it at the time.

It was a truly unfortunate turn of events that the vacuum happened to be full of glitter her coven leader had just vacuumed up after her granddaughter's visit.

It was a weird bit of magic, actually.

Pippa was quite fascinated at how her casting had turned out.

She'd wanted pastries and instead had gotten glitter.

Mounds and mounds of glitter.

The really weird thing was that the glitter didn't multiply until the vacuum was turned on.

It was probably the delay Pippa had embedded in her casting. She'd wanted the pastries to multiply only when the platter had just one pastry left. It would ensure enough pastries to last the entire meeting, but wouldn't take up too much space in the kitchen.

It was a brilliant casting, if Pippa did say so herself.

It was simply unfortunate that she somehow missed the platter and got the vacuum cleaner instead, something that didn't make a lot of sense considering the vacuum had been in a closet at the time while the platter had been right in front of Pippa.

Then again, for all she knew, the pastry spell had worked as well.

She'd been banished long before the platter of pastries had reached just one, so for all she knew, she'd left the coven with an ever-generating pastry platter, which would be entirely unfair, considering they'd banished her.

She should have taken the platter with her.

They certainly didn't deserve it!

After all, it wasn't Pippa's fault one of the witches knocked a plateful of crumbs on the floor and then insisted on vacuuming them up.

And it wasn't Pippa's fault that once the vacuum exploded, spewing glitter everywhere, no one thought to turn off the vacuum cleaner for several minutes, which resulted in ever increasing amounts of glitter exploding all over her coven leader's living room.

It wasn't like Pippa had intended that result. Besides, no one had been hurt in the rather large, repeated glitter explosions.

You'd think she'd set the place on fire the way they'd responded though. And to be clear, fire was kind of Pippa's specialty, especially when her magic was going haywire, so setting the place on fire had been a definite possibility.

Somehow though it seemed glitter was worse than fire.

All those fires she'd accidentally started over the years and not once had any of them resulted in banishment.

But explode a tiny bit of glitter, and suddenly, she was public enemy number one.

Okay, so most of the highest-ranking witches in the Coven happened to be at the leader's house at the time and had all been covered in glitter—they probably still sparkled to this day, something which gave Pippa great joy in imagining—but banishment seemed a rather harsh punishment for such an innocent crime!

Pippa had been quite upset at the time, but as it turned out, banishment had been a blessing in disguise for she was now part of a much more accepting coven.

No more witches looking down their noses at Pippa, thank you very much.

Of course, it had been difficult in the beginning, living the life of a lone witch without a coven to back her up, but then she'd met Natalie and Morana, then later, Tempest and Amaryllis.

Then they'd discovered the town of Zero and had just decided to settle there when Rowan and Jo walked into town.

In a matter of months, Pippa had somehow gone from a lone witch to one of seven and that was just fine indeed.

Except now, Pippa was bored.

Nothing ever happened in this town of seventy-three inhabitants, seven of whom were witches, and Pippa was tired of all that nothing.

The only male in the entire town who was within two decades of Pippa's own age of thirty-three was Rowan and he was a fellow witch and coven member.

Pippa had a very firm policy about witches. She didn't do them. Ever. And most definitely not witches from her own coven.

Never kiss where you plan to sleep and all that.

Which meant she hadn't had sex in about seven months now and that was a terrible record to have achieved, let alone lived through. Especially for a witch.

Sexual frustration played havoc with a witch's control, and for witches like Pippa, whose control was shaky at best, that was never a good thing.

And since she was in a coven with six other witches who were in the same boat as her, they were now a coven of extremely cranky witches with dwindling control of their magics.

Even Rowan, who had taken to driving three towns over for a little action, was starting to get grumpy.

After all, who wanted to drive two hours to have some fun, then have to drive two hours back?

"We need men." Amaryllis broke the silence at breakfast to say what they were all thinking.

Well, perhaps not Rowan or Jo.

"Uh, excuse me," Jo said. "I'd like to put in an order for eligible women please."

"Hear, hear," Rowan said.

Predictable.

Boring and predictable.

It was sad really. Seven of them and not one of them bi.

Pippa let out a huge sigh.

She really wished she was bi.

Then maybe she could reconsider her stance on no witches. After all, women were so much more reasonable than men.

"I say we cast a spell," Natalie said.

Natalie was their unacknowledged leader. She refused to accept the title of High Witch and just glared when anyone suggested she was in charge of—well, anything—but whether she acknowledged it or not, she was in fact, their leader de facto.

After all, it was Natalie who discovered Zero, a town perfect for their needs.

It was also Natalie who had paid for their rather large complex to be built. Pippa had never asked where the money came from as she figured she was better off not knowing.

Ignorance is bliss and all that, not to mention plausible deniability if the cops ever asked.

Finally, it was Natalie who'd come up with the name of their Coven, a name that never failed to make Pippa giggle.

So, yes, despite all of Natalie's objections, she was most definitely the High Witch of the Zero Cum Laude coven.

Of course, this wasn't exactly a good thing, since Natalie's magic was of the sort that kept her on the brink of madness, which made her at best unpredictable, and at worst, utterly dangerous.

"You want us to deliberately cast a spell?" Tempest exclaimed.

"Well, we are witches, aren't we?" Natalie demanded. "What are we good for if not casting spells?"

"I'm not sure this is a good idea," Morana fretted. "What if all the eligible men I call are dead?"

As far as Pippa was concerned, this was a valid fear given Morana's status as one of the strongest necromancers in modern history.

Too bad she also had zero control when using her powers.

She'd been known to raise entire graveyards, causing chaos and outrageous hours of overtime for the Witches Council and their enforcers.

It was actually quite a miracle they hadn't stripped Morana of her powers yet, particularly after her last disastrous summoning.

Pippa's theory was they were afraid of Morana's reaction should they try. No one wanted to face off against an army of zombies commanded by a witch necromancer.

"Oh, don't be ridiculous," Natalie said. "Dead people simply do not qualify as eligible."

"Depends on your definition," Morana muttered.

Pippa grimaced. She had to agree with Natalie on this one. Dead was the very definition of ineligible as far as she was concerned.

"Look, it can't be that difficult," Natalie said. "All we'll do is cast a spell asking the universe to send eligible men and women to settle in Zero."

"We chose this town for a reason," Rowan protested. "The minute you cast a spell like that, our sleepy town of seventy-three residents will suddenly become an overpopulated metropolis and we'll have to move again. There's no way we can keep our powers from revealing themselves in the middle of a city."

"So, we'll cast a spell for eligible paranormals," Natalie said. "Problem solved. Then we won't have to worry if someone notices our magic going astray."

Astray was one word for it.

Berserk was another.

Maniacally destructive yet a couple more.

"If we cast for paranormals, we run the risk of pulling other covens to us," Jo protested.

Natalie sighed. "Then we'll cast for non-witch paranormals. Can we get on with it now?"

"Hold on a minute," Tempest said. "Are we just pulling them in for a visit or are we looking for people to actually move and make a life here? Because that makes a big difference, don't you think? I mean, what if they don't want to live here, but our spell makes them stay and being a prisoner makes them so angry, they go on a murdering rampage and the next thing we know, we're all victims of a psychopathic serial killer?"

Dead silence as everyone stared at Tempest, who finally shrugged and muttered, "It could happen."

"Okay," Natalie said, drawing out the word, "so we'll cast for eligible paranormals who are seeking a new start."

"In a quiet town," Amaryllis spoke up for the first time since she'd put forth the need for men. Her head was down, her eyes trained on the patterns her fingers were making on the table's wooden surface. "A quiet town," she repeated, her voice dropping to a whisper.

Amaryllis was pathologically shy. She rarely spoke, even with them, and when she did, she never made eye contact.

"Of course, Amari," Natalie said gently. "We all want this town to remain quiet and peaceful, so we'll weave that into the spell as well."

"So," Pippa drawled out the word. "A spell for non-witch, non-serial-killing, eligible paranormals who are seeking a new start in a quiet, peaceful town."

"Exactly!" Natalie said cheerfully. "I don't know why we didn't think of this earlier." She stood and clapped her hands. "Come on, everyone. We're going to transform this town and solve all our problems at the same time."

Pippa shook her head and climbed to her feet, trying not to think of all the things that could go wrong, a list that was practically endless when considering they'd never cast a spell as a coven before.

Given how complicated this particular spell had become after one small conversation, it really wasn't the spell to start with either.

"Cheer up, Pippa," Morana said, bumping shoulders

with her. "At the very least, our days of celibacy are soon to be over. What could possibly be wrong with that?"

Great. If things weren't already destined to fall apart, that challenge sent out to the fates ensured they now were.

"We're doomed," Pippa muttered as she followed her coven outside to their circle of power.

Grab your copy of HOCUS PURRCUS today.

Other Books by Pepper

THE MURRYSVILLE COALITION

The Crazy Cheetah Lady

One Sad Kitty

A PAWSITIVELY PURRFECT MATCH

Catnapped

The Real McCat

Unbearably Cute

A Catmas to Remember

This Cat's for You

Santa Kitty

Hocus Purrcus

Tridents & Tails

Abra-Cat-Abra

Satan's Kitty

Valen-Cats

Vampurr Lovin'

A Beautiful Cat-ship

Grave Cattitude

THE SHENANIGANS SERIES

Shifter Shenanigans

Witchy Shenanigans

Full Moon Shenanigans

Hotel Shenanigans

Dragon Shenanigans

Undercover Shenanigans

Spooky Shenanigans

Holiday Shenanigans

Valentine Shenanigans

Lucky Shenanigans

STORIES OF THE VEIL

Guardians of the Veil

Astra

Glory

Luna

Zara

WICKED

No Rest for the Wicked

Wicked Is As Wicked Does

Anthologies & Collections

PAWSITIVELY PURRFECT TRILOGIES

THE CAT'S MEOW

Catnapped | The Real McCat | Unbearably Cute

HOLLY JOLLY PAWLIDAY

A Catmas to Remember | This Cat's for You | Santa Kitty

SHENANIGANS ANTHOLOGIES

CRAZED

Books 1-3

AMAZED

Books 4-6

HOLIDAZED

Books 7-10

SHENANIGANS

The Complete Collection

STORIES OF THE VEIL

THE UNVEILED

Astra | Glory

THE VEILED

Luna | Zara

WICKED DUET

WICKED

No Rest for the Wicked | Wicked Is As Wicked Does

About the Author

WWW.PEPPERMCGRAW.COM

Pepper McGraw is a USA Today Bestselling Author of paranormal romance. Her life to date has sadly been paranormal-free, but she knows it's simply a matter of time before her fated mate finally appears. Until that glorious day arrives, she keeps herself busy writing (and reading) paranormal romances.

Pepper loves animals, especially cats, and spends her free time volunteering at local shelters and for Trap-Neuter-Release programs. She's had the supreme honor of winning occasional head butts and meows from the local ferals in her neighborhood and has even convinced a few to come inside and adopt her as their own.

bookbub.com/authors/pepper-mcgraw

facebook.com/ShenanigansSeries

goodreads.com/peppermcgraw

instagram.com/peppermcgraw_author

tiktok.com/@peppermcgraw

twitter.com/peppermcgraw

www.ingramcontent.com/pod-product-compliance
Lightning Source LLC
Chambersburg PA
CBHW040534170726

48295CB00012B/460